The Painti

Sebastian was ecstatic. *She is alive! She is real! She exists after all!* The words kept repeating themselves in his head over and over again as he relived the moment when the door to the studio in Golden Square had opened to reveal the artist—*his* artist—bathed in a glow of afternoon light that poured through the windows.

A man of science and business, Sebastian had never had the least bit of patience with people who put their trust in fate, coincidence, or even the Almighty. But as the breath was being squeezed from his lungs and his heart pounded so hard that the blood throbbed in his temples, Sebastian at last acknowledged that some things existed or occurred simply because they were meant to be.

It was clear now that the recent coincidences were somehow fated to lead to her, his idealized woman, now existing in the flesh as Lady Cecilia Manners.

continued . . .

A Lady of Talent

Evelyn Richardson

A SIGNET BOOK

SIGNET
Published by New American Library, a division of
Penguin Group (USA) Inc., 375 Hudson Street,
New York, New York 10014, USA
Penguin Group (Canada), 10 Alcorn Avenue, Toronto,
Ontario M4V 3B2, Canada (a division of Pearson Penguin Canada Inc.)
Penguin Books Ltd., 80 Strand, London WC2R 0RL, England
Penguin Ireland, 25 St. Stephen's Green, Dublin 2,
Ireland (a division of Penguin Books Ltd.)
Penguin Group (Australia), 250 Camberwell Road, Camberwell, Victoria 3124,
Australia (a division of Pearson Australia Group Pty. Ltd.)
Penguin Books India Pvt. Ltd., 11 Community Centre, Panchsheel Park,
New Delhi - 110 017, India
Penguin Group (NZ), cnr Airborne and Rosedale Roads, Albany,
Auckland 1310, New Zealand (a division of Pearson New Zealand Ltd.)
Penguin Books (South Africa) (Pty.) Ltd., 24 Sturdee Avenue,
Rosebank, Johannesburg 2196, South Africa

Penguin Books Ltd., Registered Offices:
80 Strand, London WC2R 0RL, England

First published by Signet, an imprint of New American Library,
a division of Penguin Group (USA) Inc.

First Printing, February 2005
10   9   8   7   6   5   4   3   2   1

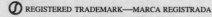
PUBLISHER'S NOTE
This is a work of fiction. Names, characters, places, and incidents either are the
product of the author's imagination or are used fictitiously, and any resemblance
to actual persons, living or dead, business establishments, events, or locales is
entirely coincidental.

For Jane Eastman,
one of the world's best reference librarians

Chapter 1

Sebastian, Earl of Charrington, frowned thoughtfully as he scanned the terms of the settlement. Certainly it was more than generous on both sides, and there was no reason to doubt that Sir Richard Wyatt would settle most of his vast fortune on his only child. For his part, Sebastian was prepared to supply his future wife with ample pin money and all the consideration the daughter of an old friend deserved, not to mention an ancient and honorable title. In fact, there really was no reason to examine the settlement except that Sir Richard would expect him to. Sir Richard would expect him to be thoroughly conversant with the smallest detail, as he had taught Sebastian to be with every business transaction that Sebastian had ever made. For, as Sir Richard had continually pointed out to his disciple over the years, it was not luck that made fortunes; it was knowledge.

It was certainly knowledge that had built Sir Richard's vast empire of mines, canals, merchant fleets, and joint stock companies. And it was knowledge, gained in a large part by learning all that one of the City's most successful men had to impart that had made Sebastian's own immense fortune. However, in this case, he already knew the terms of the marriage settlement long before they were committed to paper. There was not the slightest need to go over them again except that his future father-in-law would wish it. To Sebastian, reading a document all the way through was the least he could do for the man to whom he owed everything—the man who had been not only a mentor, but a father for the last fifteen years.

"Your coat, sir."

"Thank you, Phelps. You are quite right. It is high time I made my way to Russell Square." Sebastian slid his arms into the exquisitely cut coat of dark blue Bath superfine and waited patiently as his valet smoothed it over his shoulders and flicked away a few imaginary specks of dust.

The valet picked up his master's high-crowned beaver hat from the dressing table. "And may I be the first to offer you congratulations, sir. A most beautiful young lady."

"Thank you, Phelps. Yes, she is a most beautiful young lady."

"I am sure you will be very happy, sir."

Checking his image in the looking glass one last time, Sebastian paused as he straightened his cravat to glance at the valet. The man almost sounded concerned.

"Naturally I shall be happy."

Phelps's wizened features broke into an anxious smile as he handed Sebastian his hat. "Of course, sir. Naturally, sir."

Sebastian clapped the hat on his head, tilted it ever so slightly to a more jaunty angle, and headed toward the door. He paused as his gaze fell on the picture hanging just to the left of the door, and looked into the deep hazel eyes of the anonymous young woman who had for the last five years been bidding him adieu each time he left his chambers in Curzon Street. Sometimes her gaze was approving, sometimes it was humorous or critical, but it was always thoughtful, reflective, and oddly comforting.

Even though Sebastian had not the slightest notion who the young woman in the portrait was, he had been inexplicably drawn to her from the moment he had seen her picture in the print shop on the Strand. Then he, who had never given in to an impulse in his life, had purchased it on the merest whim.

There had been something in her expression that reached out to him that day as he had been strolling along the Strand after a busy morning at the Exchange, and he knew he had to have her regardless of price or provenance. It was a good thing he had not cared about the provenance, for the shop's proprietor had been unable to tell him much about the picture. Only that the gentleman who had sold it to him claimed it to be a self-portrait painted by a young woman who had had the very good fortune to study under the famed Angelica Kauffmann.

"Though you can see for yourself, sir, that she is a lady of some talent, to paint with such assurance at such a young age," the proprietor had hastened to add as Sebastian, taking the picture over to better light, had searched in vain for the artist's signature.

"And the gentleman who sold it to me was clearly a gentleman of exquisite taste, though down on his luck, sir, very down on his luck."

"Oh?" But Sebastian's questioning look had produced little more by way of explanation, for the proprietor had little more to offer.

"Seemed anxious to get rid of it, sir, if you know what I mean. Took my money without any, ah, discussion, except to say that it was a sad day he had returned to England, from which I gathered that he had been much abroad. Now that I think of it, he did mention that the picture was painted in Naples, but that is all I can tell you."

In fact, the lack of information about the picture itself had only added to its appeal, for it left Sebastian free to imagine whatever he wished about the unknown woman in the portrait. She was clearly a young lady of spirit as well as talent, if the slightly defiant tilt of her chin and the sparkle in her eye were anything to go by. And she was clearly not a properly raised English young lady, for there was a casualness in her dress—and in the way the mass of gold hair rioted around her face—that bespoke a freedom and a joie de vivre that would have appalled any self-respecting English miss.

It was the bright intelligence and the glint of humor in her hazel eyes that had first attracted Sebastian to the unknown young woman, but over the years, he had discovered her to be a creature of many moods. From some angles and in some lights she was thoughtful, reflective, even somber upon occasion, but she was always full of life and eager to take on whatever it had to offer her.

And it was not until now that—catching her gaze as he headed out the door to formalize his offer for Sir Richard Wyatt's only child, and the apple of his eye—Sebastian realized he had secretly been hoping all these years to find a real woman like the unknown lady of his portrait.

But there were none like her even though he had tried to find them. In all the scores of eligible young misses paraded before him by matchmaking mamas eager to secure a fortune and a title, and the numerous dashing young matrons seeking diversion with the undeniably attractive but elusive Earl of Charrington, Sebastian had never found anyone who combined wit and intelligence with the independent spirit of his unknown lady.

In the end he had come to doubt her existence himself. After all, every artist made the portrait's subject larger than life, why would it be any different with this particular painting? He had seen this phenomenon demonstrated often enough in countless exhibitions at the Royal Academy, where the season's very best portraits of the great and near great appeared more intriguing than the subjects themselves, particularly if they were female.

Sebastian climbed into his curricle, taking the reins from his tiger who favored his master with his usual impish grin. "You are looking fine as fivepence today, my lord. There's a lady involved or I'm not a betting man."

"Gambling will get you nowhere, lad." Sebastian shook his head in mock disapproval as he picked up his whip. "A

clever mind, on the other hand, will at least earn you a livelihood." He tossed the boy a shilling as Sam clambered into
his seat in the back. "You are quite right, however, though I
suspect that it is not my attire but the fact that I am taking
you along to add to my consequence, and am not headed to
the Exchange this morning that has led you to your conclusion. I am calling on a lady— a lady who is soon to become
your lady as well."

Sam let out a low whistle. "You're never getting leg-
shackled are you, sir?"

Sebastian chuckled as he flicked his whip over the team's
ears. "Yes, I am getting *leg-shackled* as you so inelegantly
put it."

"Don't do it, sir. She'll have you selling your cattle and
this curricle in no time for a coach and four. Look what happened to Lord Norwood, sir. His cattle and his rig were the
first things to go. They all want town coaches, sir, and
matched bays who have nothing but their looks to recommend them and will do nothing but sit in your stables eating
their heads off. With what it costs to feed them, she'll never
let you keep them." He pointed to Sebastian's high-stepping
grays with a despairing wave of his arm. "She'll insist that
you spend all your blunt on jewels and gewgaws for her."
Sam spoke with all the misanthropic fervor of a fifteen-year-
old orphan who had spent his formative years as a stable boy
at the Swan with Two Necks.

"I appreciate your concern, Sam, but I assure you, the
grays and the curricle are quite safe. Miss Wyatt will naturally require a carriage and jewels, but as a woman who
strives to achieve a decided air of fashion in all aspects of
her life, she will most certainly wish for her husband to cut
a dash equal to her own. It would never do for her to be married to someone possessed of inferior cattle. And believe
me, the stables at the new Grosvenor Square house are more
than adequate to keep coach horses, hacks, and my team—
all of them—in the utmost of comfort."

"I am glad to hear it, sir." Sam still looked skeptical. "But

you know women, sir. Their heads are full of romantic nonsense and they want you to dance attendance on them morning to night. You won't have time for your curricle."

"Rest assured, Sam, Miss Wyatt has no such romantical
notions. She is the most practical of women, and she herself
would scorn anyone so ridiculously sentimental as to marry
for love. Believe me. To her, romance is so much foolish
nonsense and a waste of time."

"Then she's a rare 'un indeed, sir. I have never heard of
a woman who did not want a man to spend all his time
telling her that she is the most beautiful, precious creature in
all the world," Sam observed darkly.

"Well, she is that, and she knows very well that I shall be
the envy of all men."

By the time they had arrived at Russell Square, Sam was
resigned to the fact that even heroes like Sebastian could be
rendered foolish where women were concerned. Even the
best of men could fall victim to matrimony, but at least the
curricle and the sweet-going team of grays were not to be
sacrificed. And Sam was somewhat reassured by the imposing nature of the mansion to which they pulled up. At least
his master appeared to be marrying someone who would not
bleed him dry, if the impressive nature of her father's resi-
dence were anything to go by.

Indeed, the marriage settlement was extremely generous
as Sebastian remarked to his future father-in-law as they sat
together in Sir Richard's richly paneled library. "As are
yours, dear boy, as are yours," the prospective bride's father
responded cordially. "I could not be happier for my girl than
to have her married to a man of such fine and upstanding
character as yours. It does my heart good to think that one
day this will all belong to you—for in truth, as you must
know by now, you are like a son to me."

"And a very fortunate son, indeed. I do not know how I
would have gone on if I had not run into you that day at the
Royal Society."

The older man smiled. "I knew then that you had the

makings of an excellent City man in spite of your title. It was clear to me that you had a head for figures and speculation, and I guess I was right. I usually am," he admitted, his eyes twinkling. "But figures are nothing to Barbara; it's a title she wants, and now, thanks to you, it's a title she'll have. But mark my words, she'll make you a fine countess. She has the beauty of her mother and a style and grace of her own. I've spared no expense on her education and given her the finest masters money can buy. Now all that is wanting is the proper setting to make her a leader of society, and you will give her that."

"I shall certainly try. The workmen are already installed in Grosvenor Square. All that is needed is her direction, and she may have whatever setting she desires."

"And she will most definitely give that direction, for she plans to make it the most lavishly appointed establishment in all of London, the envy of the *ton*, and one of the most frequented addresses of the beau monde. There is no stopping my girl when she sets her mind to a thing. Why, she has even made a gallant out of you, bringing you out of that hardworking shell of yours after all these years. It will do you good, too."

He chuckled at Sebastian's involuntary grimace. "I know, lad, you did what you had to do to rebuild your family's fortune and win back all that your father lost, but now it is time to enjoy the fruits of your labor, and my girl will certainly help you do that. But here"—he reached over and pulled the bell—"let us allow her to speak for herself."

He barely had time to complete his sentence before an enormously tall footman appeared. "Please inform Miss Wyatt that her father and her future husband await her in the library."

A few minutes later a vision floated into the room. Tall and graceful, Barbara Wyatt clearly inherited her lustrous dark hair from her father, but the rest of her was exquisitely feminine, from the charmingly retroussé nose to the rosebud lips and a truly elegant figure. She was the picture of fashionable femininity. "You sent for me, Papa?"

The City's most successful financier smiled indulgently at his daughter. "Sebastian and I have just been going over the settlement and, as one would expect, he has been exceedingly generous, as have I. Not only are you to be a countess, my dear, but you will be an exceedingly wealthy one. See that you use it well, for that wealth, combined with your beauty and grace will soon put the world at your feet."

"Yes, Papa." Barbara's eyes sparkled at the prospect. A bewitching dimple flashed at the corner of her mouth as she tossed a challenging look at her betrothed. "But I will count myself fortunate if my husband is at my feet. I know how you City men are, spending all your time making fortunes and none of it enjoying them. When I become Countess of Charrington I mean to make sure that both of you are seen as often at Almack's and in the ballrooms of the *ton* as you are on the Exchange, and I shall be the very picture of fashion."

"You are now, my dear."

"Papa, you *know* I am not." His daughter regarded Sir Richard with indulgent exasperation. "One is not the picture of fashion unless one is born to the Upper Ten Thousand, or marries into it." She smiled at Sebastian, whose mind suddenly seem to have wandered elsewhere.

"Picture." He murmured and than hastily banished the image of a thoughtful face framed by masses of flyaway golden hair. "A picture is just the thing to celebrate our betrothal. I shall commission a portrait of you as a wedding present."

"Splendid." Barbara clapped her hands in delight. "Sir Thomas Lawrence is a neighbor of ours, so it will be no trouble at all."

"Actually, I had not been thinking of Lawrence."

"Not thinking of Lawrence?" The look of delight faded from his fiancée's face. "But there is no one else. He has done likenesses of the prince regent, Lord Castlereagh and the queen and . . ."

"Lawrence is all very well for solemn portraits of elder statesmen and pompous peers, but there is someone new whose pictures of women at the Royal Academy exhibition were most captivating. It is a C. A. Manners, whose portrait of Lady Cowper was so lifelike that one almost felt that it was alive and breathing. In fact, there were portraits of several Almack's patronesses—Lady Cowper and Princess Esterhazy I remember quite distinctly. Surely," Sebastian raised a quizzical eyebrow, "you would not object to finding yourself among that illustrious company?"

"No, but . . ."

Knowing he had caught her attention, Sebastian continued persuasively, "In fact, now that I consider it, you do bear a remarkable resemblance to Lady Cowper though your complexion is far more delicate and your figure far more elegant—both of which will be portrayed to their utmost advantage by Manners, who seems to have a knack for capturing the very essence of his subjects.

"Besides, if one aspires to a premier position in the *ton*, it is always better to set a trend than to follow one. Everyone commissions a portrait by Lawrence; Manners, on the other hand, is still being discovered. You will have your chance to make him all the rage, which will only redound to your credit."

Sebastian knew the weakness of his wife-to-be. At the mention of Almack's most celebrated patronesses, the stubborn look vanished, and as he pointed out the possibility of setting a fashion, the sparkle returned to Barbara's eyes and the smile to her lips. "If you agree, I shall call on Emily Cowper and find out C. A. Manners's direction from her."

That settled it. Sebastian's obvious familiarity with one of the beau monde's fashionable arbiters made the choice unarguable, and the very thought of having something in common with Lady Cowper was irresistible. "Very well, then." Barbara relented.

"Never mind, Puss," her father interjected. "A woman as beautiful as my daughter—and a countess, besides—cannot have too many portraits painted of her. When you are married, my dear, I shall ask Sir Thomas to paint you in your court dress, and you will see your portrait hold pride of place in the Academy's exhibition."

Completely satisfied, Barbara thanked her fiancé very prettily and Sebastian, having finished his business in Russell Square, picked up his hat and gloves and prepared to take his leave after promising to escort his betrothed to C. A. Manners's studio once he had learned its direction. "And I feel certain that once he has seen you, Mr. Manners will drop all his commissions to paint the most beautiful woman in London." Sebastian bowed low over his fiancée's hand.

Accepting her due, Barbara smiled graciously.

Another bow, and Sebastian was off to the City, making a mental note to call on Lady Cowper.

Chapter 2

Unaware of the impending honor about to be bestowed on a relatively unknown artist, C. A. Manners, clad in a paint-daubed smock, was frowning thoughtfully at a half-finished portrait that held pride of place in the artist's Golden Square studio.

"Something about the jaw is not quite right," she muttered thoughtfully, tilting her head to scrutinize the image from another angle.

"I fail to understand why you are wasting your time agonizing over infinitesimal details," a voice spoke from a sofa that was nearly obscured by the blank canvases leaning against it.

"Oh do give over, Neville," Cecilia turned to regard her brother with an exasperated sight.

Neville Manners, the eighth Marquess of Shelburne, who was draped along the sofa, his long legs dangling over one end, as he leisurely scanned *The Sporting Magazine*, looked up from his reading. "I shall not give over as long as you remain so ridiculously obstinate. It is bad enough that you insist upon painting portraits at all, but to waste your time on a brewer? It is not at all the thing."

"Sir Jasper is a very *wealthy* brewer. And he is paying most handsomely for the privilege of being immortalized by me. Furthermore, he has a wife and several daughters whose portraits would add considerable charm to the sumptuous furnishings in either his mansion in Hanover Square or his elegant villa at Richmond. What you consistently fail to realize, Neville, is that these pictures you sneer at pay for the coats you purchase from Weston and boots from Hoby—not to mention snuffboxes from Fribourg and Treyer and cravats by the score, in addition to all the numerous household expenses you consider too plebeian even to contemplate." His sister's voice was calm enough, but it was clear from the militant sparkle in her hazel eyes and the stubborn set of her jaw that this was a topic that had been discussed numerous times before without hope of an amicable resolution.

"Expenses that you are pleased to point out at every opportunity," her brother replied. "And as *I* have told you times out of mind, you are concerning yourself over nothing. Paying tradesmen's bills is simply bad *ton*. And painting portraits for a living, for someone in our circle, is simply not done, especially if they are portraits of vulgar Cits."

"*In our circle?* Most people who have lost an entire fortune have the good sense not to try to continue to move *in our circle* as you call it. Most people would adopt the simple expedient of retiring to their estate in the country or removing themselves to the Continent."

A barely perceptible shudder shook the Marquess of Shelburne's well-knit but lanky frame. "Rustication is not my style, and the only habitable place on the Continent is Paris, where everything is just as dear as it is in London. Besides, though they may have tailors equal to ours, their bootmakers and their horses are decidedly inferior."

"We could have retured to Naples."

"*That* backwater?" Neville was horrified.

"Papa did not call it so."

"And that is hardly a recommendation for a place. The Pater held some very ramshackle notions about places, indeed—as most people who knew him would undoubtedly agree."

"Well, I do not agree. And I do not think it was a backwater, either. There was more culture to be had there, more interesting conversations—especially at Sir William's—more people of intellectual curiosity than any I have yet had the pleasure to enjoy here."

"Hamilton," her brother scoffed. "Now there was another ramshackle fellow. Artists and grave robbers grubbing around Pompeii like common laborers, and Sir William was the worst of the lot. No, it is far better to be here where I can be tolerably amused, where we're among people of our own kind, and where we can find you a husband worthy of your heritage. If, that is, you would stop burying yourself in this wretched studio with your paints and your canvases and behave like the gentlewoman you are, by cultivating the acquaintance of the proper sort of people instead of people like *him*." Neville indicated the half-finished portrait of Sir Jasper with a derogatory wave of his hand.

"Do let up, Neville, you—" his sister began, only to be interrupted by a soft knock at the door.

"Begging your pardon, my lady, but Mr. Tredlow said to bring this to you right away, as it looks rather important." The fresh-faced young maid held out a silver salver on which lay a note addressed, in a dashing masculine script, to Mr. C. A. Manners.

"Thank you, Susan." Barely glancing at the impressive seal, Cecilia tore the note open with little ceremony and, oblivious to the crest embossed on the heavy cream-colored paper, scanned it hastily. "There, Neville, you may rest more easily now, since my new patronage is bound to be rather more to your liking. This is from the Earl of Charrington asking for a moment of my time this afternoon to discuss the commissioning of his fiancée's portrait."

An impish smile hovered at the corner of Cecilia's mouth as she read further. "He says he got my direction from Lady Cowper, and from the way he is addressing me, it is clear that she has failed to enlighten him as to the gender of C. A. Manners. A very clever woman is Emily Cowper, and a very useful friend indeed."

"Charrington, eh?" Neville rose to his considerable height, yawning hugely as he stepped over his discarded magazine and headed toward the door. "A step up from Sir Jasper, to be sure, and of a good enough family, but hardly the best of *ton*. He is rich as Croesus, they say, but unfortunately, he actually earned his own fortune."

"Earned it? How novel. How did he do that?"

"Lord, I don't know. Whatever one does to earn money." The heavy sarcasm in his sister's tone was utterly lost on Neville. "Speculation in something, I suppose—the consols, annuities—I have no idea and even less interest. The man is the very devil with cards and there is no doubt that he is a very clever fellow. Bit of a rum touch, though."

"*Rum touch?* Why? What do you mean?"

"How should I know?" Neville's handsome features twisted into an exasperated grimace. "You are the one who is forever prosing on about studying character and all. All I mean is that a man who has as much blunt as Charrington does ought to be enjoying himself—ought to be at Newmarket or race meetings or following the fancy, or *something* amusing—not wasting his time in the City with as dull a set of fellows as ever drew breath. A bit high in the instep, he is—not particular cronies with anyone. They say his father lost his fortune and killed himself; perhaps it put a permanent damper on his spirits." Neville opened the door. "At any rate, he is bound to pay you handsomely for whatever he asks of you. I wish you joy of him, and now I am going to Tatt's."

And with that parting shot, he slammed the door behind him leaving his sister prey to a host of uneasy feelings—not the least of which was wondering how much her brother was likely to squander at the most famous equestrian haunt in all of England, if not the world. For it went without saying that Neville could never go anywhere, especially to Tattersall's, without parting with a good deal of *the ready*, as he so casually referred to it.

Sighing heavily, Cecilia returned to her painting. At least her reputation seemed to be growing, if the Earl of Charrington's note was anything to go by. Commissions were trickling in at a increasingly steady rate, largely thanks to the exhibit at the Royal Academy, where she had been fortunate enough to display her portrait of Lady Cowper, among others. And perhaps the Earl of Charrington, rum touch though he might be, would be sufficiently impressed by her portrayal of his fiancée that he would recommend her to his wealthy friends, even if they were a dull set of fellows. She just prayed that the future Countess of Charrington was sufficiently pretty that her portrait would be worthy of favorable comment.

In fact, Cecilia was still working steadily on Sir Jasper's portrait several hours later when Tredlow came to inform her that the Earl of Charrington and his fiancée had arrived.

"Oh Lord!" She cast a horrified glance in the looking glass that hung over the mantel. If anything, her smock was even more paint-spattered than it had been earlier when her brother had been surveying it with critical eyes, and the tendrils of golden hair that had escaped from the knot at the back of her head were now curling wildly about her face. There was nothing she could do about her hair in such a short space of time, but she hastily untied her smock, dumping it unceremoniously over a nearby stool, and did her best to smooth out the falling lace collar that was the only ornamentation on her simple round robe of primrose muslin. Ruefully, she cast one more look into the glass as the door opened. She could not help thinking how horrified Neville—who never spent less than an hour with his valet before going out—would be at her cavalier preparation. But somehow the thought of his inevitable dismay only served to amuse her and, despite her best efforts to appear as properly impressive as a member of the Royal Academy should appear, she could not stifle a wicked grin as she turned to greet her visitors.

Chapter 3

"The Earl of Charrington and Miss Wyatt to see you, my lady," Tredlow announced with as much dignified formality as if he were bringing guests into the impressively draughty drawing room at Shelburne Hall instead of Cecilia's cluttered studio. Despite the irregularity of his wages, not to mention the ever-changing, ever-decreasing grandeur of his surroundings, Tredlow never forgot what was due to the family. He served it with all the deference with which generations of Tredlows had served the Marquesses of Shelburne, despite their current reduced circumstances.

"Good day, my lord, Miss Wyatt." Cecilia held out her hand in a frank, friendly manner.

A moment of uncomfortable silence ensued as Cecilia, scrutinizing her guests' rigid faces, tried unsuccessfully to stifle another grin. "I gather that you were expecting C. A. Manners to be a Charles or a Cedric rather than a Cecilia. I admit to promoting that impression, but I assure you that I am no less an artist because I am a woman. In fact, many people—Lady Cowper among them—are of the opinion that because I am a woman I am able to appreciate and capture the essence of my female subjects far better than any man could hope to do."

"But, but . . ." Barbara was still reeling from the shock of hearing the butler say, *I shall see if Lady Cecilia is ready to receive you.* "But Charrington says that he saw your portraits at Somerset House. You cannot be in the Royal Academy. A female?" Miss Wyatt did not look as though she considered membership in the Academy to be the considerable distinction that it was.

"Why yes, I am a member of the Academy. After all, Angelica Kauffmann, with whom I studied briefly, was one of its founding members."

Barbara's blank expression confirmed Cecilia's first quick impression of her: She was a beautiful widgeon who had not the least idea of anything—especially something like the identity of Angelica Kauffmann.

Barbara turned to her fiancé. "Charrington, are you quite sure . . ."

The earl, who had been staring bemusedly at Cecilia the entire time came to his senses at last. "Clearly Lady Cecilia is an exceptionally skilled artist." He glanced at the half-finished portrait of Sir Jasper. "And"—he pointed to a rough drawing in a sketchbook that lay open on the stool next to the easel—"that is a superb likeness of Countess Lieven."

"Good heavens!" Cecilia snatched up the sketchbook, hastily closing its cover. "You must disregard that. It is the merest sketch, done the other day when she was here. She knows that I find her face to be most interesting and, as a close friend, she allows me to practice my skills while we are talking."

"It is an excellent portrait, nevertheless. It has captured the very essence of her spirit and her character as you seem to do in all the portraits of yours that I have seen. But you have a greater affinity for portraying women than men, I think." Sebastian strolled over to Sir Jasper's portrait and surveyed it thoughtfully before turning back to her.

"So I have been told." Cecilia prided herself on a scrupulous professionalism that kept her fully alive to her own artistic weaknesses, but it galled her to have them pointed out to her by this arrogant-looking gentleman who was now examining her with as critical an eye as if he were examining another one of her creations. Why should it matter to him what the artist looked like as long as the artist's skill was irrefutable? But apparently it did matter to him, for he continued to stare down at her intently, an unfathomable expression in his dark eyes.

Cecilia could not help wondering what was in his mind. Was it that he, too, like his fiancée, objected to her sex? Somehow she did not think it was that, for his face remained utterly expressionless. Yet the intensity of his gaze conveyed that it was not so much her person as her very soul that he was questioning. Again she wondered why he should care about her person or her soul as long as her work was good.

The Earl of Charrington's fiancée, on the other hand, was clearly taking stock of Cecilia's person, or at least her simple attire. Cecilia could see her mentally cataloguing the plainness of the outmoded trimmings, the signs of wear on the collar and cuffs, and comparing the entire ensemble most unfavorably with her own elegant carriage dress, which was the very latest in fashionable style and materials. It was also vastly becoming, from the triple fall of exquisite lace at the throat to the richly braided spencer cut tight to reveal a voluptuous figure, to the leghorn hat whose brim, turned up in the latest French style, framed her exquisite features, to the glossy black curls so artfully arranged to show off the perfect oval of her face and the delicacy of her complexion.

From the top of the ravishing bonnet to the tips of her green kid sandals, Barbara Wyatt was such a dazzling example of feminine beauty that Cecilia could only wonder that the earl had eyes for anything else, especially a paint-daubed artist of middling height with flyaway hair, eyes that fluctuated from hazel to green, and an unremarkable nose whose light sprinkling of freckles had stubbornly resisted applications of Roman balsam and repeated washings with Atkinson's Ambrosial soap.

But the earl continued to ignore his fiancée. "I gather,

Lady Cecilia, that you have spent some time in Naples. Is that where you acquired your artistic training? Undoubtedly that is where you must have been introduced to Miss Angelica."

"Yes, we did live there for a number of years, but how did you know?" Accustomed to studying and analyzing her subjects without their being aware of what she was doing, Cecilia was not at all sure that she liked being studied that way herself. Again, she could not help wondering what difference it made to the Earl of Charrington whether or not she had lived in Naples as long as she produced a portrait of his fiancée that would take every viewer's breath away, which was just what she intended to do.

"Your studies of Vesuvius there in the corner, the sketches of vases which can only have come from Pompeii." The dark eyes took in every aspect of the studio, from the clutter of artist's tools—palettes, brushes, stones for grinding pigments, and jars of oil—to the shelves crammed with books of all sorts, ranging from the Earl of Shaftesbury's *A Notion of the Historical Draught* to Winckelmann's *The History of Ancient Art*. "Surely that is an obvious conclusion for one to draw from the furnishings of your studio?"

Cecilia ground her teeth. Now that she thought about it, it *was* obvious, but she did not need to have it pointed out to her in that coldly superior way.

She drew a deep, steadying breath as reason reasserted itself. What did it matter to her, after all, if the man was odiously condescending? He was not *her* fiancé, thank heavens. But for a beautiful widgeon like Barbara Wyatt, he was perfect. At the least sign of difficulty or discomfort, Miss Wyatt could direct a helpless look and a plaintive *Charrington* to her lord and master and he would take care of anything and everything for her. And in all fairness, Cecilia could hardly condemn Miss Wyatt for that. For most women of Barbara Wyatt's station in life, that was the sum total of their existence—looking beautiful for the man who took care of them. Just because Cecilia refused to give over her freedom and independence to a husband—or a brother, for that matter—meant nothing as far as the rest of the world was concerned. It was Cecilia who was at odds with the rest of the world, not Miss Barbara Wyatt.

And there was no doubt about it, the Earl of Charrington looked masterful indeed, and capable of handling any situation. From the proud way he carried himself to the dark eyes that missed nothing, to the powerful shoulders and athletic frame, he was clearly a man to be reckoned with—a man accustomed to making his own way in the world. Hadn't Neville said that he had made a fortune on his own? Looking at the firm mouth and square jaw, she could readily believe it; he was not a man to be ignored or dismissed lightly. The thought of it made her own jaw lift just a fraction higher than normal. The Earl of Charrington might be a man to be reckoned with, but Lady Cecilia Manners was more than equal to the task.

"Now," she began briskly as she reached for an account book on one of the bookshelves, "what sort of portrait would you like me to paint? Full-length or half? Standing or seated? Formal or allegorical?"

Sebastian was opening his mouth to reply when Neville, a vision of sartorial splendor in a beautifully cut coat of blue Bath superfine, biscuit-colored pantaloons, and an exquisitely tied cravat sauntered into the studio.

"I beg your pardon, Cecy. I had no idea that you were expecting visitors." Utterly ignoring his sister's ironic look, he executed a graceful bow in Barbara's direction. "I hope you will forgive me for intruding, but my sister does not often entertain, especially visitors of such distinction and, ah . . . charm." He favored Barbara with a disarming smile that managed to be both reverent and frankly admiring. "I am Shelburne, by the way, and you—"

"May I present Miss Wyatt and the Earl of Charrington," Cecilia supplied, trying not to grind her teeth too audibly. Ordinarily, Neville did his utmost to ignore both her *hobby*, as he disparagingly referred to it, and her customers. Now, knowing full well that she was expecting a visitor whom Neville himself had dubbed *rich as Croesus,* he had suddenly appeared in what could only be called a suspiciously coincidental way.

"But"—Neville glanced around in horror—"can it be, Cecy, that you have offered no refreshment to our guests?" He strode over to the bellpull and gave it an exasperated tug. "You must forgive my sister," he cast a deprecating look at Cecilia, "but she is so devoted to her art that she forgets that all the rest of us poor mortals require sustenance. Why, look at me." A graceful wave of his hand called attention to a figure that could only be called willowy. "If it were not for the hospitality of our friends, I would be skin and bones, so absorbed in her work is she. Ah, Tredlow"—he acknowledged the butler with a nod of his head—"we have guests in desperate need of refreshment."

By the time Tredlow had reappeared, bearing a tray of biscuits and ratafia, Neville was regaling his sister's visitors with stories of her most illustrious clients. "Of course, having lived on the Continent, we came to be on excellent terms with Prince and Princess Esterhazy. It was on a visit to Naples that they remarked upon my sister's talent. Naturally when they called upon us here, the Prince, being a kind-hearted man, encouraged Cecy in her hobby by begging her to paint a portrait of his wife. Since then we have had a regular stream of patronesses from Almack's begging her to do their portraits as well. I keep telling her that she must stop indulging them so, or it will become a regular habit, but she insists on ignoring me. You have no idea what it is like to live with the smell of paint and turpentine." He smiled conspiratorially at Barbara as he handed her a glass of ratafia. "However, in your case, I shall make an exception to my usual objections, for clearly such beauty as yours must be immortalized. And if it means that such beauty and grace will frequent our humble abode, even for a little while, then I shall rejoice in my sister's talent, inconvenient though it usually is."

"Why, thank you." Barbara was too bemused by the patent admiration of such a dashing young man to remember that until the moment of his arrival she had been campaigning to be immortalized by an artist more universally recognized by the *ton*. But now she was considering herself fortunate to be having her portrait painted by someone whose birth and family were equal to if not greater than her skill as a painter and certainly far more illustrious than Miss Wyatt's.

Chapter 4

In fact, Barbara could not help remarking on this half an
hour later as she allowed her fiancé to help her back into
the carriage—half an hour during which Neville had re-
galed them with the latest *on-dits* gleaned at the most fashionable haunts of the *ton*. Clearly the Marquess of Shelburne
was a regular fixture at all the places which, until now, had
been quite beyond Barbara's reach. "How charming Lady
Cecilia's brother is. I have no doubt he is much sought after
at Almack's—such an air of fashion, and surely he must
dance as delightfully as he speaks. I wonder that we have
not seen him there." Barbara spoke with all the world-weary
boredom of one who had been forced to spend countless
evenings at the *ton*'s most exclusive establishment instead
of the one blissful night she had enjoyed there, courtesy of
her fiancé's aged great-aunt, who had managed to secure a
voucher for her great-nephew's future wife.

This artless speculation met with a silence so profound
that even Barbara, who was accustomed to chattering on at
length without interruption or response was moved to pause
and look up at her fiancé in some surprise. "You are so
silent. Are you quite well, Charrington?"

"What?" Sebastian roused himself from his reverie. "Er,
yes, I am quite well, thank you." He was, to be exact, not

only quite well, but better than well. He was ecstatic. *She is alive! She is real! She exists after all!* The words kept repeating themselves in his head over and over again as he relived the moment when the door to the studio in Golden Square had opened to reveal the artist—*his* artist—bathed in a glow of afternoon light that poured through the windows.

A man of science and a man of business, Sebastian had never had the least bit of patience with people who put their trust in fate, coincidence, or even the Almighty. If something could not be observed, measured, calculated, or demonstrated, then it did not exist. But as the breath was being squeezed from his lungs and his heart pounded so hard that the blood throbbed in his temples, Sebastian had at last acknowledged that there were some things that simply could not be explained by science or mathematics—some things that existed or occurred simply because they were meant to be.

Something—some unknown power—had made him discover Lady Cecilia Manners's self-portrait in a print shop that ordinarily did not deal in paintings. That same unknown power had drawn him irresistibly to the portraits by C. A. Manners exhibited at the Royal Academy, and now he knew why. It was clear that these coincidences were somehow fated to lead to her, his idealized woman, now existing in the flesh as Lady Cecilia Manners.

It was also clear, however, that C. A. Manners, or Lady Cecilia Manners as she had turned out to be, did not regard this incredible encounter as anything but a purely professional meeting. It might even have been inferred from her frosty replies to the few remarks Sebastian had addressed to her that she not only considered him simply a customer, but as an unfortunate but necessary accompaniment to the ravishing subject of her next portrait.

From the moment Sebastian and his fiancée had entered the studio it appeared that all of Lady Cecilia's concentration had been focused on Barbara—her perfect features, her graceful figure, her elegant carriage—and it had taken a good deal of effort on Sebastian's part to draw her attention to him even for the briefest of moments.

". . . most surprised to find someone of such excellent family and connections in such dowdy attire. Why one might even be pardoned for not realizing she was a lady at all if it were not for the fortuitous appearance of her brother. Poor man. It was easy to see how embarrassed he is by the casual nature of her dress and the deplorable lack of decoration in her surroundings." Barbara's voice finally penetrated Sebastian's consciousness.

"What was wrong with her attire? I thought it quite becoming: simple, yet elegant and—"

"Hideously outmoded. Why, I am sure that no one has worn sleeves like that for an age."

"Perhaps they are easier to work in. Someone who paints would not wish to have her movements constrained in the slightest degree by her clothing."

Barbara did not even deign to respond to such an absurd notion. "And to think that she is sister to a man who is so clearly alive to all that is the best in manners and costume. Did you not find the Marquess all that was charming?"

"Who? Shelburne? I thought him what he is: a most frippery fellow whose only interest in life is consorting with other frippery fellows who waste their time, talents, and money on idle diversions. He must be a trial to someone like Lady Cecilia who undoubtedly has little enough time to fritter away on such empty amusements or on fashion."

"How can you say such a thing? Why his air of fashion and his address alone would make him stand out even among superior gentlemen of the *ton*. And as to his sister, whose sense of fashion is obviously vastly inferior, I do not know why you say that it is a question of time. Why any—"

"But it *is* a question of time. A woman—or any person, for that matter, but especially a woman—who has developed her skills to such a degree that she exhibits her work at the Royal Academy is someone who is devoted to her vocation, regardless of how much natural talent she might possess. No one achieves that level of skill at anything without a great deal of work and dedication."

"Work." Barbara shuddered delicately. "One wonders why she does it, for it can only be turning her into a very dull person indeed—a veritable bluestocking—when with just a little bit of help she could be almost attractive. It is a wonder her brother allows such a thing. Surely he could use his influence to introduce her to some fashionable modiste who could make her look much more the thing."

"From the look of it, I would say that there is very little influence anyone could exert over Lady Cecilia Manners to make her do anything she does not wish to." Sebastian grinned at the memory of the defiant tilt of Cecilia's chin as she had withstood his initial scrutiny. "Besides, I think her quite pretty the way she is. There is an unaffected naturalness about her that is most appealing."

"Naturalness?" Barbara's delicate brows rose in horror. "That flyaway hair and paint all over her hands? She will never get anyone to marry her if she does not take more care of her appearance, title or no title."

"Somehow, I get the feeling that though Lady Cecilia's interests lie in many directions, none of them is matrimonial." Sebastian thought wistfully of the crowded studio filled with books and paintings, statuary and archeological treasures. What would it be like to know a woman who had led such an exciting life—a life that had taken her from England to Naples, to Vesuvius and Pompeii? What would it be like to talk to a woman who read instead of shopped, who spent hours in front of an easel instead of a looking glass—a woman whose conversation would focus on many things instead of mostly on herself?

"But it is a woman's duty to be married. How else can she look after herself? Surely Lady Cecilia is not planning to be a burden on her brother for the rest of her life? It would be most unfair of her not to exert herself in seeking out a husband."

"From the little I saw, I would venture to say that it is not Lady Cecilia who is the burden. It appears to me that she is doing quite well at looking after herself and possibly her brother as well, if her patrons number Princess Esterhazy, Countess Lieven, and Sir Jasper Chase among them."

"Sir Jasper Chase?" Barbara, who had been smiling complacently at the mention of two of Almack's patronesses looked blankly at her fiancé.

"The gentleman in the portrait on the easel in Lady Cecilia's studio."

"What has he to do with anything? No one has ever heard of Sir Jasper Chase."

"I have. He is one of the most well-regarded men in the City, not to mention a devoted patron of the arts. Believe me, his interest in Lady Cecilia's career will do more to advance it than all the others put together."

"And what woman in her right mind would want a career when she appears to be on the best of terms with people like Princess Esterhazy and Countess Lieven who can really do something to help her?" Barbara shook her head wonderingly at the sheer naivete of her fiancé. For a reputedly clever man, he could be remarkably stupid and not at all wise in the ways of the world. Her father could say all he wanted about the power exerted by the wealthy men of the City, but she knew very well that true power resided in the drawing rooms of the *ton*—drawing rooms from which she previously had been excluded, but in which she intended to play a crucial role, now that she had secured herself a place on the first rung of a ladder that was bound to lead her to more dizzying heights than her father could even imagine. And, as the Countess of Charrington, she was going to have a good deal more fun rising to the top of her world than either her father or her husband had had rising to the top of theirs.

But the first thing Barbara needed to accomplish her goal was visibility, and she was not going to get that if Sebastian continued to bury himself in his work. She simply could not allow him to continue to excuse himself from the balls and routs so necessary to her success, on the pretext that they were nothing but overheated crushes with dull conversations and tepid champagne.

No, Barbara was going to see to it that Sebastian escorted her to every affair hosted by every member of the Upper Ten Thousand, and if he would not, then she would just have to find someone else who would. Someone like the Marquess of Shelburne, for instance, someone who knew just how to cut a dash at such things, someone who knew that a person's reputation could be made or unmade by appearing at just the right place at just the right time in highest kick of fashion.

Chapter 5

Sebastian was entirely correct in thinking that Lady Cecilia Manners was doing quite well in looking after herself and her brother. However, he was not correct in thinking that she was satisfied with the state of affairs.

"Really, Neville, is it absolutely necessary for you to have *another* snuffbox from Rundell and Bridge," she asked the next morning as she stared aghast at the jeweler's bill.

"Surely you would not have me carry a Sèvres snuffbox with a striped waistcoat." Neville shuddered at the very thought of such a thing. "The clash in design would be . . . well, it simply would not do."

Cecilia bit her lip in frustration as she recorded the figure in her account book and laid the bill in the *to be paid* pile. It never did the least good to remonstrate with her brother; at best she found herself drawn into absurd discussions of fashion, and at worst she wound up being angry with him for his irresponsibility and self-centeredness, both of which were a waste of her time and energy.

Neville looked at his sister in horror. "Never tell me you are going to pay for the thing! I have only just purchased it." Seeing the mulish set of her lips, he sighed with exasperation. "Cecilia, if you are going to insist on paying tradesmen's bills, the least you can do is wait six months or more until they have sent you several dunning letters. If you do not, they will have no more respect for you than they would for some shopkeeper's daughter. Besides, if you stopped paying tradesmen, we could afford better lodgings. Golden Square may have been a respectable enough address half a century ago, but no one of any consequence lives here any more. There are nothing but foreigners here now."

"You may not consider them to be of any consequence, but I do. There are more artists, musicians, and diplomats than there were half a century ago—all people who have more of interest to contribute to a conversation than the empty-headed gossip that is usually to be heard at functions where people of *consequence* are to be found."

"And how would you know what is to be heard at such functions, since you so steadfastly refuse to honor any of those gatherings with your presence?"

Cecilia's brows rose in mock disdain. "If the *on-dits* you shared with us today are any indication of the level of conversation to be had at these functions, then I see absolutely no reason to waste my time at any of them."

"Miss Wyatt found my stories entertaining enough." Neville retorted huffily. "But then it is clear that *she* has an appreciation for the elegancies of life."

"Miss Wyatt?" His sister did not even bother to try to stifle a derisive snort. "Miss Wyatt is no more than a pretty simpleton willing to devote what little thought she is capable of to the latest cut in bodices or whatever color and material has been declared to be *le dernier cri.*"

"She at least can carry on a polite conversation. Her fiancé, on the other hand, has nothing to recommend him except his birth. If I did not already know he was of a good family, there would be no way to identify him as a man of breeding. There was none of that easy address that characterizes a true gentleman, and there was a false air of reserve about him that I found most unattractive."

"I thought it dignified. He at least had an air of distinction—cold though it appeared to be—and he certainly had

more to offer than his empty-headed fiancée. His remarks
were intelligent after all, even if they were uncomplimen-
tary," Cecilia recalled with kindling look.

"Poor creature. Miss Wyatt is such a beauty—certainly
she could have done better than that, even if he is rich as
Croesus. Surely she is plump in the pocket as well, if the stories are true. Far better for her to have found herself an
amusing man with better manners and less fortune. You cannot tell me that there are not other men of rank in London
who would not welcome a wealthy, if less-than-distin-
guished, bride."

"Why? Who is she?"

Neville smiled slyly at his sister. "And here I thought you
had nothing but scorn for gossip, Cecy."

"I wish you would not call me that absurd name." But despite her haughty tone, Cecilia had the grace to blush ever so
slightly. "It is merely that I am curious about the person
whose portrait I am about to paint. The more I know about
someone, the more I understand their character and the more
successful I am at capturing their likeness."

"And here I thought you were wondering how a highly
finished article like Miss Wyatt came to be engaged to an
old stick like Charrington."

"If you mean a man is an old stick simply because he is
not enthralled by a retelling of gossip gleaned from the
worst of the town tabbies the way his fiancée was, then yes,
you could call the Earl of Charrington an old stick—and me
as well. I, however, considered his total lack of interest to be
the one sign he had in his favor."

"Ah." Neville grinned at her. "Still, I can see you cannot
help wondering what brought this ill-assorted couple together, even though you yourself would never indulge in
anything as frivolous as speculation or the scandal broth you
accuse me of spreading. Well," he shrugged eloquently,
"have it your way. But scandal broth can be very revealing
at times and one can learn the reasons behind any number of
things, such as why a man like the Earl of Charrington is to

be wed to a woman like Miss Wyatt. It is quite simple, really: In spite of her enchanting person and equally enchanting fortune, Miss Wyatt is the daughter of a Cit. Presumably she aspires to being something more than the daughter of a Cit—like a countess, perhaps. Why she chose Charrington, of course, is anybody's guess, but I would venture to suggest that as someone who himself has amassed a fortune in the City, he has less objection to Cits and their daughters than most men of his station. And, then again, I do believe rumor has it that Sir Richard Wyatt was the one who gave him his start in whatever it was that earned him so much money. If I were so naïve to believe that such a thing as gratitude exists, I might hazard a guess that it was gratitude that made the Earl of Charrington offer to make Miss Wyatt his countess. Gratitude and a well-developed sense of . . . er . . . aesthetics. For there is not the least doubt that she will make a truly beautiful countess."

"So you do not think it a love match, then."

"A love match?" Neville snorted. "Good heavens, no! I cannot imagine how even you would come by such a gothic notion. Besides, Charrington is well known to be utterly immune to any of the tenderer emotions. Women have been casting their lures at him for years without any success. He has never shown the least interest, romantic or otherwise, in any of them. And even his, ah, *other* liaisons never last long enough to suggest any level of passionate inclination on his part. No, I fear the lively Miss Wyatt will find she has settled for a very dull dog indeed, title or no title."

"Perhaps she too is immune to the tenderer emotions." Cecilia could not say why it pleased her to discover that the vapid Miss Wyatt and her haughty fiancé possessed nothing more in common than a sense of obligation to Sir Richard Wyatt, but it did. Even though Cecilia had been irked by the earl's coolly superior air, she had been intrigued by the obvious intelligence behind it. Even more intriguing was the fact that he was not at pains to hide that intelligence as her brother's acquaintances did—if they even possessed it in the first place.

"Surely not." Again a sly smile crept across Neville's face. "As someone who has taken the trouble to understand the female mind and its motivations, I can say in all modesty that Miss Wyatt was most responsive to my obvious admiration for her person as well as for her exquisite taste. A woman who conveys that responsiveness, even as demurely and delicately as Miss Wyatt did, is hardly immune to such things. I would even venture to say that, given the right companion, she might even be . . . ah, very susceptible to those things."

"Neville! Do not even *think* of setting up a flirtation with someone who is not only my patron, but the affianced bride of the Earl of Charrington. Neville?" Cecilia's frown was thunderous. "I will not have it, do you hear me? I *will not* have it!"

Her brother laughed. "Relax, Cecy. I was merely funning. But you are positively puritanical when it comes to those ridiculous scruples of yours, professional or otherwise. You take it all far too seriously. One simply cannot help but find it amusing."

Neville yawned and glanced absently around the room. His eye fell on the hastily deposited sketchbook that lay open to the half-finished sketch of a serious-looking young lady reading a book. "There, see?" He indicated the drawing with a languid wave of his hand. Your subjects are all so very dull—wealthy Cits or raving bluestockings. There is not a speck of amusement to be found among the lot of them. Small wonder that I should find your latest subject so very attractive."

"Almeria Wolverhampton is *not* a bluestocking; she is simply a clever young woman with a quick wit and a conversation that extends beyond the latest fashions in *La Belle Assemblée.* She is a woman of interest and character, as is Dorothea Lieven whose sketch is on the page before hers." Cecilia took up her sketchbook and, closing it firmly, removed it from her brother's mocking gaze. "I like painting women of character. Capturing their likenesses offers far more challenge than reproducing the boringly symmetrical lines—or trying to instill a spark of interest in the face of—some vapid beauty."

"If you were not so preternaturally prejudiced against the Incomparables of the world, you would admit that Miss Wyatt has a lively and charming countenance. But it is clear you decided to dislike her from the outset."

"What absurdity! I neither like nor dislike Miss Wyatt. I am to paint her portrait, nothing more. What I think of her, or don't think of her, is immaterial."

Neville shot a quizzical look at his sister. Her face was flushed and her eyes sparkled with annoyance. It was unlike Cecilia to allow herself to be drawn into what she would ordinarily dismiss as a thoroughly ridiculous and time-wasting discussion. A slow grin spread across his face. "Do you know what I think? I think you are intrigued by her sober fiancé, and it irritates you to see two such unlikely people embarking on a life together. The sheer illogic of two such different people being married to one another offends your innate sense of order, and so, instead of accepting it as the way of the world, you find you must like one or the other of them, but not both. And naturally the sober, intelligent, hardworking Charrington is the one whose side you have decided to take."

"Oh do go away, Neville, and leave me alone," his sister retorted crossly. "As usual, you are being utterly ridiculous. Now leave. I have work to do." And picking up a brush and her palette, Cecilia turned determinedly to Sir Jasper's portrait.

But the brush remained poised in midair even after her brother had closed the studio door behind him. Cecilia gazed down at the small twisted tree and the few stunted rosebushes in the garden below and a pang of longing shot through her—a longing for the sweet-scented breezes and the broad blue vista of the Bay of Naples, the warmth of the

Mediterranean sun, the music and the laughter that had always surrounded her, the simple pleasures and the enlivening conversations that had been her world until the Corsican monster had forced her, her father, and her brother back to England. Would she ever return to that cherished land, even if she could never return to that cherished time? *Not if you waste the precious hours of light daydreaming like a simpleton instead of working,* a severe little voice in her head admonished her.

Sighing, Cecilia applied the brush to Sir Jasper's bushy eyebrows. The Earl of Charrington was right, no matter how nastily superior he had sounded: Her male portraits somehow did lack the vitality of her female ones. She stepped back, frowning thoughtfully as she considered why that was so. Was it because she lacked the affinity with men like Sir Jasper that she felt with people like Almeria Wolverhampton and Dorothea Lieven? Unbidden, the tall frame, high-bridged nose, and strong jaw of the Earl of Charrington flashed before her. The man's entire being exuded energy. His dark eyes, set deep under straight dark brows smoldered with a suppressed passion rarely seen in any of her brother's fashionable acquaintances—and few if any of their other friends, for that matter.

And while it was true that she preferred painting women to painting men, Cecilia suddenly found herself wishing that it was the earl's and not his fiancée's portrait she was being commissioned to paint. To be more exact, it was not strictly his likeness she wished to create, but his very essence that she hoped to capture for her own pet project, which was a series of historic paintings celebrating the mighty Samson and his epic struggles with the lion, the Philistines, and of course, Delilah.

Annoyed with herself, Cecilia shook her head vigorously to banish such silly daydreams. She had work to do, Sir Jasper's picture to finish and Miss Wyatt's portrait to begin. After all, it was not heroic historical paintings that paid their bills, but portraits, and no matter how much she longed to make a name for herself as a history painter, that would do little more than add to the luster of her reputation. For the time being, at least, portraits, and the money they brought her, were far more important than reputation.

Chapter 6

Survival, however, was not uppermost in Cecilia's mind several days later as she emerged from Turner's lecture at the Royal Academy on the perceptions of nature and the use of color. She was still so wrapped up in all that Turner had had to say on the subject that she descended the curved staircase in a fog, paying so little attention to what she was doing that had she not been holding on to the slender banister she surely would have stumbled. She started across the checkered floor of the vestibule heading toward the traffic of the Strand, and ran headlong into one of the marble columns that supported the vaulted ceiling of Somerset House's impressive entry.

"Lady Cecilia!" A deep voice tinged with laughter revealed that it was a man rather than an architectural element with which she had collided.

"I *beg* your pardon." Doing her best to overcome a sinking feeling that she knew the identity of the person she had run into, she forced herself to look up into dark eyes glinting with amusement. "What ever are *you* doing here?" Cecilia quickly stifled the irrelevant thought that when he was smiling as he was now, the Earl of Charrington was a very attractive man indeed.

Sebastian grinned. "I might ask the same of you, though

I suspect the answer would be that you have been attending a lecture at the Royal Academy. As to what I have been doing here, I have been at the Royal Society listening to what my friend Charles Babbage has to say about the calculus of functions."

"The calculus of functions?"

He laughed outright at her stupefaction. "Yes. It is a hobby of mine—mathematics, that is." Sebastian had not realized the effect their first meeting had had on him until this moment when he had her at a disadvantage. The first time, he had been overwhelmed to discover that the woman of his dreams was actually flesh and blood. He had fallen victim to her air of competent professionalism—that and her obvious intelligence and knowledge that were so evident in every corner of her studio. He had come away from the encounter feeling very dull and very provincial indeed.

It was not often—in fact almost never—that Sebastian doubted his intellectual superiority, but this woman, by her very self-assurance and composure, had somehow made him feel like the veriest schoolboy, or, at the very least, a worthless fribble who did nothing but cater to the whims of his beautiful fiancée. He had not been aware of how much it rankled until this very moment, when he took great delight in watching an uncomfortable flush suffuse Lady Cecilia's cheeks and a self-conscious look creep into her large hazel eyes.

C. A. Manners welcoming patrons to her studio was formidable indeed, but Lady Cecilia caught off guard and adorably flustered was completely enchanting and utterly irresistible. Sebastian was suddenly seized with the most ridiculous and almost overwhelming urge to sweep her into his arms and kiss the gently parted lips until she was breathless. "Yes, I find mathematics to be an absorbing distraction—a source of inspiration and predictability in an otherwise uninspiring and unpredictable world."

If she had been regarding him with mild confusion before, Cecilia looked utterly bewildered now. What had ever possessed him to admit such a thing to someone who was almost a complete stranger, a woman he had met only once before in his life?

But suddenly, and completely unexpectedly, she smiled. It was a smile that was both reassuring and intimate, a smile that made him feel comfortable and strangely lighthearted. "How interesting. I had never thought of mathematics in quite that way before. For me, being forced to do sums when I longed to read or to draw was torture. Geometry was a little better because at least it was something I could see, but algebra . . ." She shook her head in disgust. "Even Neville understood algebra better than I. But I can quite see how someone truly skilled at it would find working with numbers intriguing—like a puzzle, in a way."

"Precisely. Only it is far more useful than a puzzle. It helps one to look at the world in an orderly way, to quantify results and then see why things happen. If used creatively it can help one to think, and . . . I beg your pardon." Sebastian broke off hastily. "It is just that I have been talking equations with Babbage, and what he had to say was so inspiring that I quite forgot how dull it is to everyone else."

"No, it is not dull in the least. Incomprehensible, perhaps, but not dull." Again her smile warmed him, and touched him in a way he could not remember having been touched before. "Even I, unschooled in this sort of thing as I am, can see that such interests and skills would, for example, make you a formidable opponent at games of chance—and I am sure that is only the most obvious part of it. And now that I think of it, my brother Neville did mention that you had something of a reputation for skill at the card table."

Sebastian chuckled, oddly pleased that she had been discussing him with her brother. "Yes, actually, I do rather well at cards, but to me they are less games of chance than of probability, as are stocks and bank shares and annuities, all of which entail a good deal less risk and a great deal more reward than the toss of the dice or the turn of a card."

"Which would make cards and dice a good deal more

profitable, but perhaps less amusing for you than they are for people like my brother, who never know what to predict and thus live in a fever of expectation that the next toss of the dice or the next turn of the card will bring them a fortune."

"Or lose it." Sebastian fell silent. The amusement faded from his face, and a look that could only be described as bleak crept into his eyes.

Her curiosity piqued, Cecilia held her breath, waiting, wondering what memories or thoughts were responsible for that faraway expression.

Then he seemed to collect himself. His lips twisted into an ironic smile. "I myself find the most intriguing part of it all to be the calculation of the odds, but I admit that my interests are rare to the point of being peculiar. For most people, as you so aptly observed, it is the fever of anticipation, the endless possibility, that drives them to such an extent that it hardly matters to them if they win or lose. And they generally lose."

This time there was no mistaking the bitterness in his voice or the bleakness in his expression. Inspired by an impulse she could not fathom or explain, Cecilia laid a gloved hand on his arm. "And I gather that you know someone who lost. I am sorry."

Again he felt the oddest urge to confide in her. He did not know whether it was the warmth of understanding in her eyes or that he had become so accustomed to addressing his innermost thoughts to her picture that willed him to do so. Almost without his being aware of it, the words came pouring out.

"Yes, I did know someone like that: my father. He never met a game of chance he didn't like, though faro was his preferred means of wasting his inheritance. He spent most of his time at the gaming tables of White's, and then in less savory establishments as his obsession grew and his fortunes declined. My mother and I rarely saw him until the day he came riding home on a borrowed horse to tell us that he had finally lost everything, even the roof over our heads. And then he went out in the fields and shot himself. They found him the next day when the horse wandered into a farmer's barn with my father still on his back. Unfortunately for us, he was the second son, so we had no entail to protect us and we were forced to throw ourselves on the mercy of his brother, the earl—as cold and selfish a man as you could ever hope to find."

Sebastian paused for a moment. He rarely, if ever, spoke about this part of his life to anyone, and he could not imagine why he was doing so now, except that she seemed to understand everything he was trying to convey. At any rate, he had told her the worst of it, and there was no point in holding back now. He swallowed hard and continued with his story.

"As someone who had elected to live a bachelor existence, my uncle was not best pleased to have a destitute widow and her son suddenly thrust upon him. He accepted his new responsibilities begrudgingly. I was quickly banished to school, while my mother became little better than his housekeeper. It was a miserable existence, for he was a dreadful miser and mean-spirited to boot, but it did not last very long—for my mother, at least. Worn out with worry, and overwhelmed by the shame of my father's death, she soon wasted away to an early grave.

"It was small consolation to me when my uncle died unexpectedly the very next year. I inherited the title, but very little else, for, as he said in his will, leaving me a fortune would only encourage me in the spendthrift ways of my father. He left all his money to the Church—a place he had little enough contact with in his lifetime, but which he found useful for spiting me in death. I was left with the estate, for he could not will that away from me, but not the wherewithal to run it properly. His niggardly ways had left it in such desperate shape that it has taken me years to restore it properly. It did, however, provide me with enough income so that I did not have to be a scholarship student at Cambridge, which would have made me a total outcast. As it was, the fellows at school avoided me because of the unsavory circumstances surrounding my father's death."

Knowing very well what it was like to scrimp and save after an improvident parent's death, Cecilia nodded sympathetically.

"Fortunately for me, however, the isolation I had endured at school had turned me into something of a scholar and I did rather well at university, which, while it did not make me popular with the bulk of the students, did win me friends among the like-minded ones.

"By the time I graduated, I had gained enough of a reputation for cleverness that I was able to find a position in the City, where men are rewarded for their talents rather than their social standing. The men who rule the City do not care what one's father did or did not do; they only care for the skills one possesses. But by the time I had reached that more forgiving and congenial society, I had been forced to rely on my own resources for so long that I no longer cared one way or another whether they accepted me socially, just so long as they accepted me professionally. There is nothing so cruel as the taunts of fellow schoolmates or as brutal as the way they treat anyone who is set apart from them, especially by misfortune, and I learned early on that it is a rare person who will stand as your friend if you are different from the rest."

A lump rose in Cecilia's throat at the thought of the poor lonely little boy he must have been. "The orderliness of mathematics must have been most reassuring to you. I do hope that you were able to take some comfort at least from being able to apply yourself in an area where your success depended only on you, and not on the superficial likes or dislikes of other people or the fickle nature of society."

Overwhelmed by the sympathy in her eyes and the simple joy of being understood, Sebastian raised her gloved hand to his lips. "You are a woman—no—a *human being* of rare understanding, Lady Cecilia. Small wonder you are such a talented artist. You see through to the souls of your subjects, and you capture them in your painting."

It was Cecilia's turn to find herself at a loss for words. Nothing in a very long time had made her feel as appreciated as Sebastian's simple, heartfelt words of admiration. And it had been years since anyone had held her hand—not since she had been a little girl climbing the hills overlooking the Bay of Naples with her father. She had forgotten what it felt like, the touch of another human being, warm and reassuring, and infinitely comforting.

"Oh my lady, I do beg your pardon. I hope you have not been waiting long, but the man in the shop took an age about his business." A young maid, cheeks flushed with exertion and very much out of breath came hurrying up to the earl and Lady Cecilia as they stood there in the vestibule.

"Do not worry, Susan. I have only just got here myself." Cecilia was both annoyed and grateful for the interruption. Her latest subject's fiancé was having an oddly disturbing effect on her, and while Cecilia might allow, or even encourage, her imagination to take over when she was painting, she was not about to do so in her own life. Up until the moment Susan had appeared, she had been dangerously close to letting that happen.

Chapter 7

The trancelike state of warmth and intimacy that had come over Cecilia when Sebastian had taken her hand in his was not easily banished, despite her best efforts to focus her thoughts elsewhere. Much to her disgust, Cecilia spent the entire ride home thinking over the conversation they had shared in the vestibule of Somerset House.

Who would have thought that a man engaged to a shallow beauty like Barbara Wyatt would exhibit a profound interest in anything—especially something as intellectually rigorous and demanding as mathematics? In fact, the more she considered it, the more Cecilia was forced to revisit her original opinion of the Earl of Charrington, and to ask herself if the man she had dismissed so easily as cold and arrogant was perhaps as deep and complicated as the field in which he had expressed so much interest.

While Cecilia had welcomed her maid's sudden appearance, and had been glad of an excuse to end a conversation that threatened to involve her more closely than she had any desire to be, Sebastian, on the other hand had done his best to prolong it. He had even offered to take them home in his curricle, insisting that he had nothing better to do with his time—no other destination in mind than a certain house in Golden Square.

But the more he had insisted, the more Cecilia had re-solved to take a hackney as she had originally planned until at last, smiling ruefully, Sebastian had given in. "Very well. I shall not insult your intelligence any further by claiming that I have not a single obligation today; but believe me, none of them is so important that it begins to compare with the pleasure I would take in furthering our conversation. However, I can see that you are not only very determined, but also very independent, and, as someone who values his own independence highly, I cannot in all conscience press you to change your mind, though I am sorry that you won't."

He did, however, help her into the hackney, retaining her hand in his for a few moments longer than was absolutely necessary. "Thank you for a most enjoyable conversation."

The words were wholly inadequate for the message he wished to convey—his sense that he had just discovered the rarest of treasures, someone who truly understood him—but he was forced to be content with them. He ground his teeth in frustration as she took her seat, but as he looked into the hazel eyes gazing down at him, he saw that somehow, miraculous as it was, she seemed to comprehend all that he was trying so hard to make her understand.

"I enjoyed it too." Cecilia replied so softly that he had to bend close to her to catch her words. And then, before he could say or do anything more, the carriage began to roll forward, its driver eager to take advantage of a break in the press of traffic on the busy thoroughfare.

Regretfully, Sebastian closed the door and stood there watching as the carriage made its way up the Strand. And it was not until it had completely disappeared from view that he realized his own curricle was right there as well, with Sam waiting for him expectantly, a hint of impatience in his stance.

Hoping he did not betray how sheepish he felt at being caught staring like a mooncalf after a departing hackney, Sebastian took the reins from his tiger and climbed in. But even as he negotiated his way in front of a cart horse that took great exception to the curricle's very presence in such a commercial area, Sebastian's mind lingered over the conversation with Cecilia.

How could he have gone on about himself in that nonsensical fashion when there was so much he wished to know about her? Where had she learned to paint with such power and skill? Why was it that she, a gently born young lady, was now apparently supporting both herself and her brother by painting portraits? How was it that a young woman of such obvious intelligence, determination, and talent, had a brother who equally obviously possessed none of these characteristics? And why had Sebastian never met her before?

The answer to the last question, he suspected he could provide for himself. From the little he had seen of Lady Cecilia Manners, it seemed relatively safe to assume that she had as little inclination for frequenting the fashionable haunts of the *ton* as he did, and, given their mutual lack of interest in such things, it was not surprising that they had never encountered one another.

Fighting the almost overpowering urge to drive after her and put these questions to her immediately, Sebastian forced himself to head in the opposite direction of Golden Square toward Change Alley and the congenial distractions to be found among the patrons of Garroway's coffeehouse. Perhaps the negotiation of a few canal shares or the purchase of an interest in a water company would take his mind off the intriguing question of Lady Cecilia Manners.

Lady Cecilia had played a big enough role in his life when she had been nothing more than a portrait on the wall, though it had not been obvious to him how big a role she had played until the day came when he had made his formal offer for the hand of Miss Wyatt. Heading out the door, he had met the portrait's gaze and it was then that he had become blindingly aware of all the silent conversations he had shared with it, all the unuttered confidences he had entrusted to it over the years that it had graced his rooms in Curzon

Street. But now that he had discovered that the lady of the portrait was actually flesh and blood, she had become far more than a mere confidante. She had become a real threat to the very essence of Sebastian's well-ordered life.

An unknown lady who happened to embody all the characteristics of his ideal woman, his ideal companion, was one thing. She could be admired from afar without requiring any involvement on his part. Furthermore, her shining example could make all others—the real women he encountered in his daily life—pale in comparison so that they had no real effect on him whatsoever. Thus he had been able to insulate himself from all of them, remaining comfortably immune to the charms of even the most beautiful and enticing women who vied for his attention. He had even been so arrogant as to congratulate himself on having avoided all the inevitable pitfalls and traps of romantic entanglement that had plagued the rest of his acquaintances.

But now that Sebastian knew his lady of the portrait was a real person, there was no avoiding the effect that she had on him. Worse yet, everything he had since learned about her, every word that had come out of her mouth after the initial shock of the introduction, had only served to confirm that his ideal companion did exist and that she was Lady Cecilia Manners. But what in God's name was he to do about it?

As Sebastian drew his team to a halt in front of Garroway's and handed the reins back over to Sam, he came to the unnerving realization that he had been very comfortable in his previously held belief that his ideal companion did not exist. In fact, this belief had given him the protective isolation that had allowed him to focus all his energies and attention on other things. While other men—his competitors in the financial world—had had their attention diverted and their time taken up by lovers, mistresses, and wives, Sebastian had been able to forge ahead single-mindedly, secure in the belief that he was, and always would be, alone in the world. No one had ever truly understood him or even cared about him when he was growing up, and there had never been any compelling reason to believe that life would ever change. Until now.

Now he did not approach Garroway's with his customary anticipation. Now the warmth of the smoke-filled room and the comforting hum of dozens of speculative financial discussions no longer compelled him to come home. He had experienced the warmth of sympathetic understanding in someone else's eyes, known the comfort of a compassionate smile, and shared his story with a person who not only could appreciate it, but who also appeared to share much of his outlook on life.

And for the first time in his life, Sebastian, who had come to feel at home in the risky but rewarding world of the stock exchange, now wished he were somewhere else. He wished he had insisted on escorting Lady Cecilia back to her studio in Golden Square. He wished he were sitting there now on the sofa by her easel, talking about her paintings, discussing the books that crammed the shelves, and learning as much about her life as he had told her about his. Clearly, her life had been even more unusual and adventurous than his had been, and it had certainly produced an unusual and adventurously self-reliant woman.

"Charrington, I was hoping to find you here. Saves me from having to send a footman over to Curzon Street." A firm hand gripped Sebastian's shoulder, and he turned to see his prospective father-in-law smiling jovially at him.

"Come join us over here, lad." Sir Richard indicated a group of men gathered at a table in the back of the room— not Sir Richard's customary table in the corner, but a more discreet setting away from the crowd.

"There are some fellows here who would like to talk to a man warm enough in the pocket to take a considerable risk, and farsighted enough to appreciate the rewards that can be reaped from a daring venture. The proposed scheme they have for lighting up the city of London should appeal to a man like you. And, as a man of science, you are better able than most to evaluate the validity of the proposed scheme."

Sebastian sighed inwardly. The distraction he had hoped for had just arrived. Why, then, did he not welcome it? Ordinarily his prospective father-in-law was one of the few men he was always happy to see, but at the moment, Sir Richard's appearance only reminded Sebastian of his daughter, and the woman who was to paint her portrait.

As he followed Sir Richard through the crowd to the table, Sebastian wondered idly what Lady Cecilia, a woman who possessed intellectual taste, would find to discuss with his fashion-mad fiancée. For surely there would have to be some sort of conversation between the two of them in order for Cecilia to understand Barbara's distinctive personality and convey it on the canvas.

Did Barbara in fact *have* any character? Sebastian wondered as he nodded to the men seated at the table. Certainly she was strong-minded enough, and not the least bit shy about expressing her likes and dislikes, but did she possess anything more than a decided preference for the latest Egyptian-inspired furnishing over the more restrained classical style of Adam, or an inclination toward the high-crowned Angoulême bonnet rather than the flatter one favored by the Duchess of Oldenburg? But neither of these previously articulated tastes revealed anything more about Barbara Wyatt than an unerring instinct for placing herself in the setting most likely to show off her striking attributes to their very best advantage.

Chapter 8

Several days later, Cecilia was wondering much the same thing as Barbara Wyatt draped herself gracefully on a damask-covered bergère that Cecilia had positioned to catch the warming rays of the afternoon light streaming in through the windows at the back of the studio. Certainly the Earl of Charrington's fiancée possessed both the wit and taste to select the gowns and the pose most likely to display her figure and her fact to the best possible advantage, but did she possess anything more?

As Cecilia began to sketch out the first outline of the sitter's beautifully sculpted features, she very much doubted that there was anything more to Barbara Wyatt than a sense for presenting herself to the world in a way designed to capture the most possible admiration and attention.

It was not that Barbara Wyatt was dull or stupid. It was quite the opposite, in fact. She was a fountain of information, all of it useless, and she kept up such an inexhaustible flow of inconsequential chatter that Cecilia longed to shout at her to be quiet, except for the fact that it gave her a wide range of facial expressions to choose from. And she was certainly clever enough to know how to arrange not only her surroundings but the people around her to her best advantage.

Finally, however, the flow appeared to be slowing and Cecilia, heaving an inward sigh of relief, stepped back to look at her handiwork. She frowned in concentration for a moment and then moved forward, her chalk poised to add further definition where it was needed.

"Are you quite certain that you have caught my best angle?" Barbara lowered her chin a fraction of an inch. "There, this shows the becoming tilt to my nose which I vow is more charming than Lady Cowper's. I must remind Charrington to tell her that when we next see her at Almack's." She paused as though struck by an interesting thought. "How is it that I have not seen you there, for I know you have painted several of its patronesses? In fact, it was Charrington's forceful representation of their consistent patronage that convinced me to sit for you in the first place. Was it at Almack's that you became acquainted with Lady Cowper and Countess Lieven? I vow I consider Almack's to be the most charming place in the world. Do you not think it so?"

"Actually, I do not." Cecilia was not at all sorry to admit it.

"What? Not adore Almack's? How could one *not* like the most important gathering place of the *ton*?"

"I do not dislike it, precisely. I just find it difficult to carry on any sort of intelligent conversation there—and since conversation is the only possible reason for attending a social affair, there is really nothing to draw me to the place when I can use my time more profitably elsewhere."

"You sound just like Charrington." Barbara pouted prettily. he is forever telling me that the refreshments are dull and the company even duller, but now that we are engaged, I shall make sure that he escorts me there every week. It will be good for him, for *he* is the one who is in danger of becoming dull, not Almack's. Why, he is as bad as Papa. All the two of them ever do is work. It is a wonder he even got the notion into his head to marry me, for all he ever thinks about is shares and annuities and the wretched consols. I suspect that Papa suggested the match, for he knows I intend to become an Incomparable, which one cannot really hope to do without a title. I am glad Papa suggested it, however, for I think it will be vastly amusing to be the Countess of Charrington, don't you agree?"

"I expect it will." Cecilia rubbed her forehead wearily, leaving a black smudge just over one eyebrow. The lady's incessant chatter was beginning to wear on her nerves, but she had learned one thing, at least: the impending marriage between the Earl of Charrington and Miss Wyatt was definitely not a love match, nor even, it appeared, a long-standing arrangement. Why she found that reassuring, or why she should even care, Cecilia did not know. She only knew she was glad the earl—whose conversation revealed him to be a man of some intelligence—had not fallen under the spell of someone who was as empty-headed as she was beautiful.

Fortunately for Cecilia, the sound of her brother's voice told her that she was saved from having to pretend further interest in her subject's conversation.

"In the studio with Miss Wyatt?" Neville's voice echoed up the stairs. "Very well, I shall have a glass of Madeira in there." And with those words, Cecilia's brother strode breezily into the studio. "Oh,"—he turned back towards the hall and shouted down the stairs—"and bring some refreshment for the ladies."

"Miss Wyatt." Neville flashed a devastating smile, and executed a bow in the sitter's direction. "How delightful to find you here. What could be more refreshing after an exhausting session with my tailor than to find myself in the company of such a charming visitor as you? It quite makes me forget the rigors of the morning. Consulting with Weston is less arduous than working with anyone else, mind you, but even he requires a good deal of direction. One cannot be too careful with these things, you know."

"I quite agree." Barbara was all smiles and sympathy. "The hours I spend with Madame Céleste are beyond anything, but if one is not careful with these people, one can find oneself clad in last year's fabric or—worse yet—last year's color. One simply cannot spend too much time over these things, for one's clothes are the face one presents to the world."

"Now if we could only convince my dear Cecy of the importance of such things . . ." Neville shot a teasing glance at his sister, whipped an exquisitely white handkerchief from his pocket, and wiped the smudge from her brow. "But she will tell you that our exteriors should be the merest reflection of our souls, and therefore we should expend all our efforts on our own characters rather than on our accoutrements. Have you ever heard anything so absurd?"

Neville stepped back to observe the nearly completed sketch and nodded approvingly. "Very like. You have outdone yourself this time, Cecy. But then, you have a subject who is inspiring, instead of some dull old brewer or branfaced bluestocking. Still, there is nothing like the original, which I find I infinitely prefer to the copy. Tell me, Miss Wyatt, will we see you at Almack's this week?"

"But of course! Where else would anyone be on a Wednesday evening? Anyone who is anyone, of course."

Neville shot a sly glance at his sister. "Cecy would not be there if she could help it, would you, Cecy? There, see how she frowns like a thundercloud at me? When a gentleman cannot count on his own sister to keep him company at Almack's, what is he to do? I trust, Miss Wyatt, that I may at least count on you to stand up with me? For now that you have sat for your portrait in our humble abode, I consider you to be as close as any of our acquaintances."

"Oh, my lord, you do flatter me." The faintest of blushes crept into Barbara's cheeks as she fluttered her lashes in a way that managed to be both modest and seductive. "You are so kind. It is always delightful to be reassured of having one partner at least."

"What? Surely your fiancé has already claimed the first and the last dances?"

Barbara's lips drooped as she shook her head.

"This is dreadful! Why, if I were Charrington, I should claim *all* your dances, scandalous though it would be. How could he lead anyone else to the floor when his wife-to-be is the most exquisite creature in the world?"

"Oh, he does not lead anyone to the floor—not me, not anyone." Though Barbara might complain about the social failings of her fiancé, her pride drew the line at appearing pathetic. "He thinks dancing is merely an excuse for people to avoid intelligent conversation."

"In this case, Miss Wyatt"—Neville smiled at her sympathetically—"I think I must agree with your fiancé. To a certain degree, dancing is often a replacement for conversation, but that is not necessarily a bad thing. When one finds oneself with a partner as lovely as you, one prefers to admire rather than converse. Then, of course, there are those partners with whom one stands up simply because one must, and then one is most grateful for relief from conversation. However, you and I shall enjoy ourselves on the floor and leave my sister and your fiancé to converse to their hearts' content. There now, Cecy, you see? You must come to Almack's with me this time so you can converse with Charrington while Miss Wyatt and I indulge ourselves in something less serious."

A derisive look from his sister was the only response Neville received to this last sally. He grinned broadly. "You see what a hopeless case she is, Miss Wyatt? Your fiancé, at least, goes to Almack's even if he does not dance. My sister, on the other hand, does her level best to avoid it altogether. She considers it to be a deplorable waste of her time."

"But what could be a better use of one's time?" It was Barbara's turn to smile sympathetically at Neville. "Everyone who is anyone is to be found at Almack's. It is where all the best marriages are made."

"And my sister will be happy to inform you that she is not interested in marriage, Miss Wyatt." Neville shook his head sadly.

"Not interested in marriage? But *everyone* is interested in marriage!" Eyes wide with astonishment, Barbara turned to Cecilia. "But what will become of you? How will you go on?"

Cecilia chuckled. "Nothing will become of me. I mean that I shall carry on the way I do now, I expect. I shall continue to paint and have my studio. Naturally I hope to become more skilled at what I do, and advance myself as an artist, but as to the rest . . ." She waved airily at her surroundings. "I have what I need, so I shall continue on as I have begun."

The very thought of it was too much for Barbara, who looked at her in dumbfounded silence.

Neville chuckled. "So now, Miss Wyatt, you understand why all my efforts to introduce her to good society have had so little effect on her. The only way I can possibly convince her to come to Almack's with me is to assure her that it is good for her reputation to be seen where there are so many lovely women worthy of having their beauty captured for posterity in a portrait. But if she deigns to join me there, she will certainly not waste her time on such frippery as dancing." He executed a slight bow and tossed an appealing look in Barbara's direction. "I hope I can convince you to stand up with me for at least one dance, and even possibly two." His gaze dwelt on her admiringly. "I am certain that someone who carries herself as gracefully as you do also dances exquisitely, and I look forward to it. But now, if you will excuse me, Sefton is counting on me to be his partner at whist."

Another quick bow to both of them, and Neville was gone, leaving his sister to stare after him, a decidedly speculative expression in her eyes.

It was not her brother's sudden departure that aroused Cecilia's suspicions, it was his appearance in the studio in the first place. Usually Neville did his utmost to avoid spending any time at all in surroundings he considered to be beneath his station in life. So why had he bothered to stop in between his appointment with Weston and his afternoon at the gaming tables at White's? There was only one answer that presented itself: Miss Barbara Wyatt.

That morning at breakfast, when Neville had mentioned his appointment with the *ton*'s premier tailor, he had taken instant exception to the disapproval he had read in his sister's eyes. "But Cecy, a gentleman must have a few rags to his name; otherwise he is simply not a gentleman."

"Certainly. But I just paid Weston's bill, and I am quite certain that it included a blue jacket of Bath superfine."

"Of course it did, but one cannot show up in the same attire day after day. Speaking of which, I ought to accompany you to Bond Street and see to it that you find some toggery for yourself." He cast a disparaging eye over her morning dress of lavender sarsenet, which was plain to the point of severity. "Look at you! Not an ounce of lace or ruching, and a color that went out of fashion quite three years ago. If you are not to look a complete dowd, you must have something in lemon or primrose muslin. I insist on taking you to Madame Céleste's myself, for that is the only way we are going to get you rigged out in proper attire."

"And pay for it how?" Totally unimpressed by this generous offer, his sister had turned her attention back to *The Times,* which she had been perusing before he had appeared at the breakfast table. "Besides, Miss Wyatt is coming for her first sitting today and I must make sure that everything is all in order."

"Ah, the beauteous Miss Wyatt" had been her brother's only comment, but there had been a gleam in his eye that, coupled with his unexpected appearance in her studio later that afternoon, now seemed decidedly suspicious.

But Cecilia, busy putting the finishing touches on her preliminary sketch of the lady in question, had no time to dwell on the question of her brother's erratic behavior. "There." A few more strokes to add definition to the chin and Cecilia stepped back, well satisfied with the day's work.

She turned to Barbara. "I believe that I now have enough to begin painting. I shall send a note around to you when I am ready for your next sitting, but I believe I should not have to do that for at least a week."

Barbara rose and, drawing on her gloves, smiled slyly. "But surely I shall see you and your brother a good deal before that."

Cecilia stared at her blankly.

"At Almack's. After all, your brother has claimed at least one dance with me." Barbara smiled, serenely confident in her belief that the combination of Neville's persuasiveness and the allure of Almack's would overcome any nonsensical objections that Lady Cecilia might raise to what she would undoubtedly consider an evening wasted in London's most celebrated assembly rooms.

Chapter 9

Left in peace to begin serious work on her latest commission, Cecilia found herself unable to plunge into the project. Her thoughts kept returning to her earlier conversation with the portrait's subject. How was she to capture the essence of Miss Wyatt for posterity if, in fact, there *was* any essence, much less the character and spirit that Miss Wyatt's fiancé considered to be the hallmarks of a portrait painted by C. A. Manners?

Cecilia studied her sketch thoughtfully. There had to be *something* more to Miss Wyatt than her undeniable beauty and her obsession with all things fashionable. Surely there was something there besides the obvious—something deeper that had attracted and held the attention of a man like the Earl of Charrington.

Cecilia was still mulling over her unexpected encounter with the Earl at Somerset House. At the end of their first meeting, she had ultimately and reluctantly admitted him to be a man of intelligence, or certainly keen powers of observation. That concession in and of itself had been difficult enough, for she would have preferred to dismiss him as simply a wealthy, quietly elegant man of the world and nothing more. But there had been something about Sebastian, Earl of Charrington, even at that initial introduction that had drawn her to him and made her uncomfortably aware that he was a man to be reckoned with.

Their subsequent meeting had only served to strengthen her first impression. Now Cecilia was not only drawn to him, she was intrigued by him. Not only was he a clever and astute observer, which he had proven almost immediately, he was a man with a soul—a man who had suffered the isolation of being an outcast in a very rigid society and come to terms with it, a man who had made a success out of the talents that had set him apart from his peers, a man who was not so different from herself in his drive, his ambition, and his independence.

Cecilia felt heat rise in her cheeks as she remembered the way his dark eyes had bored into her the first time he saw her, and then later, the glow of appreciation and even intimacy that had warmed them as he raised her hand to his lips. No, the Earl of Charrington was not so different from Lady Cecilia Manners, he was remarkably similar—disturbingly so.

And it was time to stop thinking about him and concentrate instead on his fiancée. Cecilia bit her lip so hard that it hurt as she forced herself to focus on the delicate oval of Miss Wyatt's face, the large brown eyes, the slender nose, the firm little chin.

There was no doubt that it was an enchanting face, but . . . Cecilia's mind went back to their previous conversation and she could not help chuckling as she recalled Barbara's look of horror when Cecilia had declared herself to be uninterested in marriage. Her eyes had gone from Cecilia to the crowded little studio and back again. To a woman like Barbara, accustomed to the most luxurious surroundings money could buy, it was inconceivable that anyone could be satisfied with anything less.

That was it! Cecilia grabbed her chalk and began filling her rough sketch with the finer shadings of character. It was Barbara's very obsession with fashion and society—her drive to be a diamond of the first water and a leader of the *ton,* her refusal to accept anything less for herself than the position of an Incomparable, despite her damaging connections with trade—that made her who she was and, to some extent, gave her a certain dignity of character.

Heaving a sigh of relief, Cecilia, put chalk to paper and worked furiously until the fading light forced her to stop, sit down, and take a drink of the tea that Susan had brought her nearly an hour earlier. But tepid though it was, the tea revived her. After lighting the candles, she went back to her work.

The warmth of the candlelight bathed the room in a golden glow, softening the surroundings—hiding the clutter of brushes and pigments, the stacks of books and papers in the shadows—and making the room appear cozier than it was during the day. Cecilia glanced around with a sense of peaceful satisfaction. No, it was not luxurious, but it was her place. She had told Barbara that she wanted nothing more, which was mostly true. However, her innate honesty forced her to admit to herself that this was not entirely true.

What she truly longed for—though most of the time she would not allow herself to admit it—was her light, airy studio overlooking the Bay of Naples—the water glittering a brilliant blue in the warm Mediterranean sun, the scent of orange blossoms wafting in through open windows. Even more, she longed to see her father in the chair opposite her, studying her sketchbooks with the half-critical, half-proud expression that he reserved for her and her alone. How she missed him!

A lump rose in Cecilia's throat. No, she would not think about it. It did no good to think about it. Those days were gone forever, never to return, and she should count herself fortunate to have experienced them. She should also count herself fortunate that she had her art to support and sustain her, that she had no need for anyone to watch over her, or care for her. She did not need anyone else's criticism or appreciation; she had herself for that.

Those days might be gone, but they were not forgotten,

and the very next day a most tangible reminder of them appeared in Cecilia's very own studio.

"A gentleman to see you, my lady." Tredlow barely had time to announce the visitor before he ushered in a handsome-looking gentleman of medium height whose expressive eyes and prominent nose lent an air of sensitive intelligence to his smiling countenance.

"Signor Canova!" Cecilia exclaimed in delight as, snatching up a handy rag, she wiped off her paint-daubed fingers. "How very happy I am to see you! Do come in. I have been thinking longingly of Italy—Naples especially—on this gloomy day, and you are like a ray of sunshine, a welcome reminder of those happiest of days."

"Ah, the Marchese di Shelburne, your father—how much we miss him! Such a clever, amusing man and warm companion. It is to his friendship that I owe the many connections that now bring me here. But I still miss him, as I do you, my talented young friend. I hear great praise of your work, here in London, Signorina Cecilia. Your papa would be very proud."

"You are too kind, Signor." Cecilia smiled gratefully at him. "But see for yourself."

The sculptor stepped forward to take a closer look at the evolving sketch of Barbara Wyatt. "You are struggling with this one, I see, Signorina Cecilia. There is great beauty there and the beginning of a sense of the person underneath." He pointed to the detailed rendering of the nose and chin. "But the eyes, though lovely, are empty." He shrugged. "No matter. I know you. You will work and you will work, and in time you will get it exactly right. Still," he glanced over at the recently finished canvas of Sir Jasper, "you are busy, I think, and that is good."

"Yes, that is good, though they are only portraits, and not the paintings I truly wish to do."

Canova raised a sympathetic eyebrow. "So young and so impatient. These things take time, my dear. Even Signorina Angelica was forced to paint portraits to survive, despite her reputation as a history painter. Do not worry: Sooner or later all those hours you spent copying the sculpture and the ruins, the paintings of the Italian masters, will ultimately convince the critics that you are capable of working on greater things. And, now that I am advising your government on the purchase of Lord Elgin's marbles, as well as executing a few commissions for your prince regent, I am in an excellent position to remind them all of your considerable talents for painting history as well as portraits."

Cecilia smiled gratefully. "You are too kind. But tell me, how have you been enjoying London?"

The Italian's eyes lighted up. "It is a most remarkable city! Such wide handsome streets and squares, so clean, so . . ." he searched for the words, ". . . so very prosperous. And everyone has been so kind—the prince, the queen, the Landsdownes, the Hollands . . . Oh, everyone has kept me exceedingly busy and exceedingly well entertained."

"Not so well entertained, I hope, that you will not be able to join me on Sunday. There are a number of artists living nearby, and we hold informal conversazioni at one another's studios. This Sunday it is my turn to host our little group." Cecilia shot him an impish look. "It would indeed be a feather in my cap if I could offer the possibility of your presence as further enticement to my guests."

Canova laughed. "But of course. Anything I can do to further the reputation of one of my favorite artists." Then his expression grew sober. "It is rather like the old days, is it not? The congenial conversation, the fellowship of artists, and the pleasure of good company. I still miss your papa's afternoon gatherings at the Villa Torloni."

"As well as those at the Palazzo Sessa. We sorely felt the lack of Sir William when he returned to England, but Papa did his best to carry on the tradition."

"Signor Hamilton was a good friend and a most important patron. We are all indebted to him." Canova agreed.

They spoke for some time of mutual acquaintances and shared memories of Cecilia's life in Italy, as well as the projects on which they were both working. In fact, it was not until Tredlow came to announce the arrival of another visitor that Cecilia realized they had been chattering away for the better part of two hours.

"The Earl of Charrington," Tredlow announced in stentorian tones, as though he were leading the visitor into the most impressive of drawing rooms instead of an artist's cluttered studio.

"*O Dio!* Look at the time!" The sculptor rose hastily as he caught sight of the bracket clock in the bookcase. I must be going. I promised Lady Holland I would call on her today and the afternoon is almost gone. You are too charming a companion, Signorina Cecilia. It is far too easy to lose all track of time in your presence."

"I hope I do not interrupt," Sebastian began hesitantly.

"You are not interrupting anything, my lord." Cecilia could not think quite why she was so eager to reassure him of this, except that the Earl of Charrington, despite his broad shoulders and imposing height, looked oddly forlorn at having discovered another visitor in her studio. "In fact, I am delighted to present Signor Canova to you. He is one of our oldest and dearest friends, and I am happy to say that business with our government has at last brought him here to London."

Canova bowed and smiled at Sebastian in the friendliest of fashions. "It is a great pleasure, my lord. But indeed, I believe that we are not total strangers, for my friend Sir Humphry Davy often speaks of you as one of the cleverest men in the Royal Society. In fact, if I am not mistaken, I saw you when I was there with him the other day."

"Ah yes, of course." Sebastian relaxed so visibly that Cecilia wondered what it was that had made him appear so hesitant in the first place. "You are the one who was so helpful to him when he was in Rome last year. Actually, it is his recent discussion on the nature of the pigments used in the frescoes at Pompeii that is responsible for my visit to Lady Cecilia today. I am no chemist, and naturally I would not even begin to compare myself to Sir Humphrey Davy, but after reading his paper, 'Some experiments and observations on the colours used in painting by the ancients,' I did some research of my own that I thought might be of interest." Sebastian's words were addressed to both of them, but his eyes were all for Cecilia.

And there was no mistaking the expression of admiration in them or the flush that stained Cecilia's cheeks. Her other visitor watched the entire exchange with avid interest, and hastily stifled a sly smile that crept across his lips.

"How very kind of you to think of me." At last Cecilia found her voice. "I am afraid I am but a poor scientist, however. You will find me sadly ignorant where such technical matters are concerned."

"And that is utter nonsense." Canova edged imperceptibly toward the door. "Lady Cecilia is one of the most clever women it has ever been my pleasure to meet. But now, I fear that I am expected by another clever lady." He turned to Cecilia. "You will be delighted to know that she has been a great contributor to our cause."

Seeing Sebastian's puzzled expression, Cecilia hastened to explain. "In addition to advising the government on the marbles it is considering purchasing from Lord Elgin, Signor Canova is raising a subscription to return the works of art plundered by Napoleon to their rightful owners."

"A truly Herculean task." The sculptor shook his head sadly. "But thanks to patrons of the arts everywhere, we are slowly succeeding. Or, as in the case of this courageous lady here, we managed to rescue them before they were stolen to grace the emperor's various residences, and those, it was easy to return. But now I truly must bid you adieu, though I look forward to your Sunday conversazione." And with the briefest of bows, Canova hurried from the room, congratulating himself on having introduced a topic of conversation designed to increase the earl's patent admiration for the lovely and talented C. A. Manners.

Chapter 10

"I hope you will pardon me for asking how you aided in Signor Canova's cause, but I feel sure that there is an interesting story behind it, and my natural curiosity will not let me pass it up." Sebastian looked down at Cecilia with a smile that was somehow irresistible.

"Oh, I did not do anything much." Cecilia's knees, which seemed to have become oddly unreliable in the earl's presence, now threatened to give way entirely. Gesturing to a chair on one side of the fireplace, she sank into the one opposite it, hoping desperately that she looked grateful rather than overwhelmed.

"I simply agreed to take some of the pictures in danger of being plundered with me when we were forced to leave Naples. It was easy enough to remove them from their frames and stretchers and roll them up inside some of my own paintings."

"I agree with Signor Canova; you are a courageous woman indeed."

"Nonsense." Self-consciousness made Cecilia respond more tartly than she intended. "There was not the slightest bit of danger. No one would think to notice, let alone question, a young girl."

"Perhaps," he admitted. "Nevertheless, while you might

not have been in any actual physical danger, you acted on your principles by taking up a noble cause and helping to advance it. Very few people have the strength of mind, much less the will to do anything that would discommode then, let alone expose them to difficulty or even discomfort. You are a very different person from your brother, I think."

"What?" Thrown off guard by this unexpectedly prescient observation, Cecilia could only goggle at him stupidly.

Sebastian chuckled. "Of course, it is the merest guess on my part with hardly a shred of evidence to support my theory, other than the most casual observation, but I imagine that the two of you often find yourselves at loggerheads."

Cecilia nodded ruefully. "Yes, I am a great trial to Neville, for try as I might, I simply cannot find it in myself to cultivate the interests that every properly brought-up young lady does her best to cultivate. I fear that making a splash in society is not a sufficiently compelling reason for devoting my entire day to embellishing my appearance. You see"—an impish twinkle sparkled in her eyes—"I am really no different from those people of whom you spoke so slightingly just now, for I do not discommode myself either, nor expose myself to the discomfort or difficulty of spending hours in front of the looking glass deciding on just the right coiffeur or poring over the illustrations in *La Belle Assemblée* so that I can then endure torturous hours of fittings with the dressmaker. I enjoy my comfort just as much as anyone else."

The minute the words were out of her mouth, Cecilia regretted uttering them. A man accustomed to escorting the always fashionable Miss Wyatt was bound to compare the carelessly put together Lady Cecilia Manners most unfavorable to his exquisitely turned-out fiancée.

But that did not appear to be the case. Far from being horrified, Sebastian appeared to be highly amused. He chuckled softly. "On the contrary, Lady Cecilia, you are artist enough to know that your person needs no embellishment, that simplicity becomes you and is always more elegant than whatever absurdity happens to be the latest kick of fashion. Furthermore, you have the courage to be who you are rather than ape the latest fashion plates in the hopes that your finery will serve to define you to the rest of the world."

"Why . . . why, thank you." Not for the first time, Cecilia wondered how a man possessing the unique sensibilities the Earl of Charrington appeared to possess was affianced to the eternally à la mode Miss Wyatt. "But as you so rightly guessed, my brother would disagree with you, though he is kind enough not to fault me entirely for being such a dowd. Much of the blame he lays at Papa's door."

"Oh?"

"Neville says it is all on account of my irregular upbringing, and that I might have turned out quite properly if I had been raised in a normal way."

"I am afraid that I must disagree with Neville, for it appears to me that you have turned out quite properly indeed. However, I will admit that it is most unusual for me to enjoy anyone's company as much as I enjoy yours, so it is therefore safe to assume that yours was an unusual upbringing."

"I suppose it was. Mama died when I was very young so I have no recollection of her. Papa could not bear to remain in a place that was filled with so many memories, and he was never interested in running the estate or taking his seat in Parliament. In addition to that, he always admired the work of his friend Sir William Hamilton so we moved to Naples very soon after Mama died, when I was still very young. Of course, I always had various nurses of sorts, but no proper governesses. Papa always insisted that the conversations of his friends were far more enlightening and edifying than anything he had ever heard uttered by a governess, and that I would do better to model myself after them than try to learn any of the standard female accomplishments that any governess worth her salt would insist on instilling in me."

Cecilia paused for a moment, staring ruminatively at a

small picture of the Bay of Naples. It was a night view illuminated by a full moon, with the ominous glow of Vesuvius in the background. "I suppose that, in many ways, what Papa was doing was raising a friend for himself. His acquaintances were so many and so varied that they could teach me more than any governess, and a surprising number of them were women. One was a protégée of the famous anatomist Signora Manzolini, who gave me a far greater understanding of that subject than most men possess—a subject that is of critical importance to any painter, and one in which most female painters are woefully ignorant. But there were others too—scientists and philosophers from Bologna, where women of talent and intellect are not so looked down upon as they are here. I will admit, however, that I preferred my lessons in drawing and watercolors to anything else."

"You were most fortunate in your father; it sounds a most fascinating upbringing to me."

Sebastian's wistful tone and his obvious envy made her smile. That this wealthy and undoubtedly powerful man should envy a young woman who was barely able to support herself and her brother by painting portraits was more than a little absurd. "It might seem that way to you, perhaps, but Neville loathed it. He longed to be at a proper school with his proper peers. I, on the other hand, reveled in the freedom of learning anything and everything that interested me, with no one telling me it was time to stop with one sort of lesson and take up another. However, Neville is correct in being critical to a certain degree, for I am woefully ignorant in areas that do not interest me. A true governess would never have allowed that to happen."

"But you are exceptionally skilled in others. A true governess might not have allowed that to happen either." Sebastian leaned forward, his elbows on his knees, chin in his hands—the very picture of informality that Neville would have found utterly appalling. "Tell me about how you came to be interested in painting."

Cecilia shook her head slowly. "I do not actually recall a

time when I was not interested in it. From the earliest moments I can remember, I was drawing. And Papa always encouraged me." She smiled reminiscently. "Of course, he did not allow me just to scribble away according to my fancy. As soon as he saw that I had some facility for it, he sought the advice of friends. He was an artist of some natural ability himself, but no training, which he always regretted. So from an early age I was set to copying the styles of the masters, sketching the antique vases in Sir William's collection, and reproducing friezes and paintings from the ruins at Pompeii and Herculaneum. I was extremely fortunate in my surroundings. One could hardly help becoming an artist when surrounded by so much beauty, both natural and manmade."

It was the faintest of sighs, quickly stifled, but he heard it. "And you miss it."

Cecilia looked up, her eyes stinging with unshed tears. "Desperately."

Sebastian's heart turned over at the sadness in her voice and the unabashed honesty of her answer. More than anything, he wanted to give back to her what he imagined to be the camaraderie and easy pleasure and enjoyment of those sun-filled days. "And what happened?" He prompted gently.

"Napoleon." Somewhat ashamed of revealing so much of herself to a man who was little better than a stranger, Cecilia grimaced ruefully, striving for a lighter touch.

He chuckled. "The man who can be credited for laying waste to any number of idyllic situations. So you wrapped up your paintings, along with a number of them that you were saving from the greedy clutches of the Corsican monster, and fled."

"Yes. And we came to London because Papa still could not bear to return to Shelburne Hall."

"I imagine that Neville, at least, was pleased to be home."

"Ecstatic. But Papa was miserable. He found society here to be intolerably dull and confining after the free and easy interchange that was the norm in Naples. He used to complain that everyone looked and sounded the same, with their long, pale, disapproving faces and no variety, no laughter, no true gaiety whatsoever. Slowly he lost his gaiety as well, and simply wasted away. Well," her innate honesty forced her to add, "I should say that he wasted everything away."

Something in his eyes, a flash of sympathy and comprehension, compelled her to continue. "He was dreadfully bored, but rather than deadening his senses with drink as so many do, he sought to stimulate them by gambling. At first it worked. He seemed more alive, told me that at least he was using his wits again. But then it too began to bore him. He became careless and, well . . ." She smiled bitterly. "You can guess the rest. He began to lose, so he spent even more time at the gaming tables trying to win it back. Soon he was neglecting to eat or sleep. He grew thinner and more frail, so that when he contracted an inflammation of the lungs after walking home in the rain one night, it was only a matter of days before he succumbed."

Sebastian's eyes were fixed intently on her face as her narrative drew to an end—on the hazel eyes glittering with tears, the brows that frowned so fiercely in an effort to keep those tears from spilling down her cheeks, the straight nose with its sprinkling of freckles and the delicately sculpted lips that quivered in spite of her best efforts to still them. And as he stared at her, he slowly began to see another face—an older face whose lines of laughter had turned to lines of cynicism and despair, whose eyes had lost their spark and were haunted by desolation, a face tanned by the Italian sun. The Marquess of Shelburne, her father, the man Sebastian had helped to ruin.

His insides twisted painfully as recognition dawned. How could he have been such a fool? Of course the jaded and desperate gambler had been Cecilia's father. It was just that for so long he had thought of her as C. A. Manners, and then Lady Cecilia Manners, that he had remained oblivious to the connection. Naturally, Neville was now the Marquess of Shelburne, but Sebastian had so quickly dismissed

Neville as such a monstrously shallow piece of fashionable inconsequence that he had hardly paid attention to his name or his title.

A cold wave of something midway between guilt and disgust washed over Sebastian, leaving him weak with apprehension. What had he done? And what was he going to do now? He could not avoid telling her. After all, it had been her innate honesty that had drawn him to her in the first place—her determination to live her life the way she wanted to, to look at life in the face and choose her path according to her interests and not society's expectations, regardless of the consequences. And admiring her for being true to herself, how could he now choose the path of deceit?

On the other hand, how could he bear to tell her the truth? How could he admit to being a party to that slow wasting away she had so eloquently described? And the worst of it was that he could not plead ignorance. No, Sebastian had been fully, vitally, intensely aware of what he had been doing. He had been punishing a man for giving up on everything, giving up on his family and his responsibilities, ignoring everything in order to pursue the hypnotic lure of the gaming table just the way his own father had.

Never mind that Sebastian had put all the money he had won from the Marquess of Shelburne into a fund for destitute widows and their children; he now knew that he had destroyed the one person it seemed that Cecilia loved beyond all others—the man who was not only her father, but her teacher, her mentor, and her friend. How was he ever going to make it up to her?

By doing nothing, a cowardly little voice inside him insisted. At least not for now. He would wait. He would become her friend, her patron, her champion. And over time, he would study how to make it up to her, and in time he would. He swore himself to it with all the fervor he had sworn to recover his own father's lost fortunes. But in the meantime, he needed to learn as much about her as he could so that in return he could give her everything that she had ever wanted.

"I am so sorry."

Cecilia shrugged dismissively. "Now you see why I knew so well how it was with your own father, only I turned to art rather than to mathematics to sustain me. And I turned to my work in order to make me forget."

The sympathy in her voice was a knife to his heart. Her acknowledgment of their shared sorrow making it twist until the pain was almost more than he could bear.

"And to give you a growing reputation among the connoisseurs of fine portraiture," he added. The lightness of his tone seemed miserably contrived, but he could think of no other way to extricate himself from a sea of emotions that threatened the very core of rational aloofness with which he had protected himself all these years since his father's death.

"Yes." She grimaced. "I suppose so."

"And you do not find that gratifying?"

Cecilia raised her chin ever so slightly, a tamer imitation of the defiant glare she had given him during their first meeting when he had made the unfavorable comparison between her male and her female portraits. "To the extent that I find it gratifying to be considered a skilled craftsman." She sniffed disdainfully. "But where is the artistry in that? I would be a poor creature indeed if I did not aspire to anything more than that."

Sebastian grinned in spite of himself. Never before in his life had he encountered someone as driven as he was. It was like discovering some long-lost kin—a brother, a sister . . . or perhaps his ideal companion. "Then am I to take it that history painting is your true calling?"

Cecilia looked at him with considerable respect. It was a rare person indeed, even among artistic circles, who could appreciate the difference. "I hope it is. But I have not tried it enough to know."

The mixture of legitimate pride in her skills coupled with her innate modesty was as disarming as it was enchanting.

Sebastian could not help himself. He wanted to know more and more about her. He wanted to listen endlessly, to watch the expressions follow one another across her mobile face, to see her eyes sparkle with amusement and darken with intensity, the lips go from soft smiles to firm determination, the dark brows quirk up with irony or knit with intensity. "And why have you not tried it?"

"I cannot earn a living at it, and I must earn a living."

It was a simple enough statement, uttered without shame or complaint, and Sebastian could not think of anyone he knew or knew of—man or woman—who would have admitted to such a thing with such natural dignity. Most people in the Upper Ten Thousand did their best never to mention money at all. It was simply not good *ton* to acknowledge its existence, much less a need for it. "I see. And portraits allow you to earn a living?"

"Yes, they do. It is not that I dislike portrait painting precisely." Cecilia hastened to add. "But if one is really going to make a name for oneself as an artist, it must be as a history painter. And I intend to make a name for myself as an artist."

Again, it was a simple statement of fact, and Sebastian could not help being inspired by her quiet confidence and her determination. "Then I shall try to do my best to see that you do."

"You?"

He had answered her without thinking, without realizing how patronizing or how ridiculous it might sound for a man of business with very little, if any, true understanding of art, to offer to advance her career. He had only known that he wanted her to have her heart's desire, and he had only been thinking of what he could do to help.

"Yes. If you will let me. I believe I have a project that might be of some interest to you. If you have the time, I mean."

Cecilia stared at him. It was hard to believe that a man like the Earl of Charrington—a man so accustomed to making his own way in the world—should sound so tentative, so hesitant. If she did not know better, she would almost have said that he was unsure of her approval, but such a thought was ridiculous. Still, she could think of no other explanation, and she liked him the better for it.

But for the moment, it was more than she could take. She was already dangerously close to sharing more of herself with this man than she had ever shared with anyone, even her father, and it made her decidedly uneasy. All her life she had struggled to become independent. She had learned from her father's example that nothing and no one could be depended on, and she was not about to begin to do so now, especially with a man who had a far more demanding and attractive female who required his complete and constant attention.

Smiling, Cecilia rose and held out her hand. "Thank you. It is most kind of you to take an interest in my career, but it is really not necessary."

In the face of such a clear dismissal, Sebastian could do nothing but rise as well and take his leave. But he did not want to. He wanted to remain comfortably ensconced in her cozily cluttered studio talking about her hopes and dreams. He had never felt so close to, so completely comfortable with, another person in his entire life—so at ease, so utterly at home—and he hated to have it come to an end, even for a moment.

Chapter 11

It was not until Sebastian was seated in the gaming room at Brooks's later that evening that he realized he had never given Cecilia the paper on pigments that had been his ostensible reason for calling on her in the first place. He had been so distracted first by the presence of Signor Canova and then by the discussion of her life and her dreams for its future that he had completely forgotten about it until now.

It was not like him to be so stupid. Sebastian scolded himself for his lapse. He rarely forgot even the smallest of details. In part, it was his ability to keep track of a multiplicity of details while still remaining focused on whatever issue was at hand that was responsible for a good deal of his success in the City—that coupled with his phenomenal memory and his talent for figures.

But all those skills seemed to be fading away now that Lady Cecilia had entered his life. Or, to put it more accurately, now that he had blundered into hers. For compared to her rich and varied past, his seemed like the merest of existences bounded by his travels from Curzon Street to Change Alley, and enlivened only by the occasional lecture at the Royal Society or an evening at the theater. And how very dull she must think him after having been raised in the com-

pany of artists like Kauffmann, Canova, and amateur ar-
chaeologist Sir William Hamilton.

Sebastian envied the sculptor and his casual references to
Cecilia's Sunday conversazione which sounded as though it
was one of those gatherings of interesting people bent on
seeking out intelligent conversation that had been such an
integral part of her childhood and her education. It was not
the intellectual stimulation Sebastian envied, for he could
certainly find that at the Royal Society, as much as it was the
informal camaraderie. What would it be like to be surrounded by a circle of friends with whom one shared such
similar interests that one looked forward to getting together
with them on a regular basis?

"Ahem, are you still with us, Charrington?" His partner's
voice broke in on Sebastian's reverie.

"Thinking, Trevelyan, just thinking." Sebastian frowned
at the cards in front of him and hoped desperately that the
rest of the players attributed his lapse in attention to strategy
rather than woolgathering. He took the trick with a trump
and forced himself to concentrate on the hand in front of
him.

But somehow the game failed to offer the challenge and
diversion he sought. Giving up in disgust, Sebastian left
early, hoping to clear his head with the stroll home.

The crisp night air did nothing for him either, and he soon
found himself sitting in his chair by the fire, meditatively
sipping a glass of brandy and staring at Cecilia's portrait.

She could not have been very old when she had painted
it, yet there was a gravity in her expression even then that
showed her to be a young woman of great determination as
well as talent. Talent was all very well and good, but without the will to succeed and an ever-present goal in front of
her, she would never have achieved a place for herself in the
Royal Academy's exhibits, or what appeared to be a steady
stream of commissions for portraits.

Sebastian admired that will tremendously, which was
why he had mentioned the possibility of a project to her—a

project that just might further her in her chosen career of becoming a history painter. Tonight, however, as he looked at her portrait, he found himself wishing that he could give her some enjoyment in life, as well as success.

And what did she enjoy? Not the usual round of routs and balls that were the stuff of most young ladies' dreams. Both Cecilia and her brother had made that infinitely clear. Intelligent conversations with like-minded individuals appeared to be something she sought out, but she already had her conversazione.

Sebastian's eye fell on a copy of *The Times* he had tossed onto a table earlier that day. Of course! The theater. He had been so busy lately that his box at Covent Garden had sat empty more often than not. He riffled through the pages until he found the theater announcements. *A School for Scandal* might not appeal to a woman whose bookshelves included Tasso and Ovid as much as Shakespeare would, but surely it could not fail to divert her for an evening. Having seen Cecilia and her brother's adequate but modest lodgings in Golden Square, Sebastian felt it safe to hazard a guess that their finances were limited, as least as far as Cecilia was concerned. The exquisite fit of the Marquess of Shelburne's coat, the immaculate whiteness of his cravat, and the boots that could have only been made by Hoby made it clear that her brother felt himself under no similar economic constraints. As a man of business, however, Sebastian was well aware that it was far easier to ignore dunning letters from tradesmen than from a landlord, and thus, their lodgings were a far more accurate indicator of their financial status than Neville's accoutrements—a financial status that probably did not allow for much indulgence in the theater.

The more he thought about it, the more Sebastian decided that he might as well confer enjoyment upon himself at the same time he was offering it to Cecilia and her brother. It had been an age since he had seen Sheridan's play. Furthermore, it was a play whose plot was such that even his frivolous fiancée was likely to find herself tolerably amused.

But when he broached the subject to Barbara during a drive in Hyde Park at the height of the fashionable hour, she was not in the least bit interested. In fact, if the tragic droop to the lips that more than one besotted swain had compared favorably to a rosebud were any indication at all, his fiancée was not only disinterested, she was highly displeased. "Really, Charrington, how could you?"

"But I thought you would be pleased that I am not *wasting* my time on business or in the card room at Brooks's as you so often accuse me of doing."

The beauty softened, but only a little. "I am. But it is a Wednesday evening."

His blank look only exasperated her further. "Really, Charrington, even *you* should know better than that. We will be at Almack's."

"Oh." Sebastian did his best not to shudder at the daunting vision of Wednesday evenings for the rest of his life filled with meager refreshments and even more meager conversation. "But, my dear, now that you are suitably affianced—at least, I hope you consider yourself to be suitably affianced—surely there is no need to subject yourself to the rigors of the Marriage Mart."

His fiancée cast him a pitying look. "And Papa considers you to be one of the cleverest men of his acquaintance. Honestly, for a clever man you are remarkably buffle-headed. Now that you have made your fortune, have you stopped going to Garroway's and the Exchange and left it all to chance? There!" She smiled triumphantly. "You see? Maintaining one's position in society is no different than maintaining one's position anywhere else."

Sebastian sighed. His wife-to-be was not clever in the standard sort of way. Her interests tended toward the shallow and frivolous, but where her own well-being was at stake, she often demonstrated an undeniable quick-wittedness that never failed to catch him off guard. "Very well. I fully acknowledge the error of my ways, and shall endeavor to escort you to the best of my poor abilities."

Barbara tapped him playfully with the ivory handle of her parasol. "I shall make certain it is included in our marriage vows, and then you are assured of remembering. Besides, I shall not require you to dance more than one or two dances with me, as I promised to save one at least for the Marquess of Shelburne."

"The Marquess of Shelburne will be there?" Sebastian hardly dared hope that the modish Neville would be able to prevail upon his reclusive sister to accompany him to the mecca of the fashionable world, but even the possibility that he might gave Sebastian hope that there might be at least one person who could offer him companionship among the marriage-mad misses, their equally marriage-minded mamas, the gossiping town tabbies, and all the other assorted social arbiters who attended that most exclusive and dull of gatherings.

"He would not miss Almack's for the world, or the opportunity to dance with someone he swears is destined to become all the rage," Barbara confided happily.

So it was, that, dutifully leading his fiancée to the floor on the evening in question, Sebastian kept a weather eye out for the Marquess of Shelburne's lanky but elegant figure, and was quickly rewarded by the sight of his blond head towering above Lord Alvanley, with whom he was deep in conversation.

Doing his best to maneuver them closer to the pair, Sebastian was astounded to see the Marquess of Shelburne's sister standing at his elbow.

In spite of the others who crowded around Alvanley in the hopes of overhearing one of the celebrated wit's bon mots, Cecilia appeared to remain emotionally aloof from the crowd. And as they approached, Sebastian noticed from his partner's self-satisfied smile that even though Cecilia's gown of pink satin trimmed with blond lace was exceedingly becoming, it must not be in the latest style.

Barbara, who could always be counted on to be in the highest kick of fashion, was wearing a white satin slip over a white lace dress whose décolletage made Cecilia's look positively modest, while her headdress of pearls was in decided contrast to Cecilia's simple knot of hair with only the golden curls clustering on her forehead to call attention to her expressive eyes.

Still and all, though there was no doubt, as always, that Barbara was stunning in her beauty, there was a vulnerable yet sensual quality about Cecilia that made Sebastian long to hold her in his arms, feel the softness of her hair against his cheek and the warmth of her skin under his hands. Perhaps it was the very lack of ornamentation that made him so supremely aware of the woman underneath—the smoothness of her skin, the silkiness of her hair, the delicacy of her long, tapering fingers as she brushed aside a stray curl and surveyed the crowd with the distant gaze of someone who clearly felt herself to be an observer rather than a participant in the fashionable charade taking place around her.

Sebastian grinned in spite of himself as a wave of relief washed over him. He had found a friend, someone who was as ill at ease, as bored, and as frustrated with the entire scene as he was. And quite suddenly the air did not feel so claustrophobically stuffy or the laughter and the chatter so irritatingly intrusive as it had only moments ago.

"You did say that you had promised a dance to Shelburne, did you not," he asked hopefully as their set ended.

Barbara nodded.

"And here he is. I feel certain that I can convince his sister to sit the set out with me while the two of you take to the floor." And with all the aplomb of a man who knew how to go about getting whatever he set his sights on, the Earl of Charrington guided his fiancée easily through the crush of people, who were so intent on hearing the conversations of their neighbors or casting critical eyes on the costumes of those around them, that they parted easily in front of him without even being aware that they did so.

Chapter 12

"Miss Wyatt, your éclat this evening casts all others into the deepest shadow." Neville greeted Barbara and her fiancé with the most elegant of bows. "Truly, Charrington, you are the envy of every man here. I predict that in no time at all your wife-to-be will become one of the high priestesses of fashion, and you will find yourself looking longingly back on the days when you were able to lead her to the floor without being crowded aside by scores of eager aspirants."

"La, my lord, you are far too gallant." Barbara's gratified smile betrayed her to be in complete agreement with Neville's gracefully articulated sentiments.

"Then I must take advantage of this opportunity to lead you to the floor, for once I have done so and the *ton* has seen you with a partner who does you justice, I shall never be able to do so again without having to fight for the privilege." He held out his arm to her and she took it happily.

Sebastian's lips quivered as he glanced over at Cecilia. But the Marquess of Shelburne's sister was made of sterner stuff. Years of listening to her brother's idle chatter had inured her to even his most outrageous compliments. She merely raised a quizzical eyebrow as she murmured, "That is praise indeed, even from Neville, for he sets the very highest of standards, you know. It took the greatest act of courage on his part to enter these hallowed portals holding the arm of a woman whose gown is quite two years out of date."

Sebastian chuckled. "I am impressed that he convinced her to make her appearance here at all."

Cecilia made a moue of disgust. "He caught me in a weak moment."

"And here I thought that Lady Cecilia Manners never suffered from such a thing."

"Not ordinarily." She could not help smiling back at him. There was such a wealth of sympathy and understanding behind the teasing glint in his dark eyes. "However, Neville did point out that I had not quite got the eyebrows right on your fiancée and that the quickest way to rectify that was to join him here this evening, where I would have ample opportunity to observe her face in a variety of expressions."

"Not got the eyebrows right? I should have thought that would have been done easily enough."

"Neville maintains that they are extremely expressive and I have utterly failed to appreciate that fact."

"Hmmm. Does he now?" The earl stared thoughtfully at Barbara and Neville who were now whirling gracefully around the floor.

"In this particular case, I do believe he has a point."

Sebastian smiled down at her. "And are you always so enchantingly devoid of hubris, Lady Cecilia?"

She colored fiercely, not so much at his words as at the way he looked at her. The warmth of his admiration felt as intimate as a kiss, and it left her oddly shaken. "I . . . er . . . I don't know what you mean."

"Come now, Lady Cecilia. You are clearly a superior creature to your brother in any number of ways, and you just as clearly bear very little respect for his way of living, yet you refuse to dismiss his opinion out of hand simply because you cannot respect the rest of what he stands for. I find that as admirable as it is rigorous. It shows the mark of a true artist — one who is willing to learn whatever she can, regardless of the source, just so long as it improves her art."

"Why . . . why, thank you," Cecilia responded slowly. She tilted her head to one side as she considered his words. "I had never thought of it that way, but yes, I suppose that is what I try to do; learn wherever and whatever I can from whomever I can."

"Then I hope your coming here tonight has been worth it. I was not so sure of that when I first caught sight of you. You looked as thought you wished desperately to be almost anywhere else but here."

"Did I?" She laughed. "I am afraid I am but a poor dissembler. My face has always betrayed my thoughts far too readily for my comfort."

"I am glad of that." Watching the sparkle in her eyes and the dimple that occasionally peeped out at the corner of her mouth when she smiled, Sebastian wanted desperately to think that she was enjoying herself now, at this moment, in his company. "But why do you dislike it here? Most young women would trade their souls to be seen here at the Marriage Mart."

"That is because most young women aspire to nothing more than to be married," she responded tartly.

"We have certainly established that you aspire to a great deal more, but surely you do not rule out marriage?" Sebastian had not the least notion why he had allowed the conversation to stray to such a personal topic. Ordinarily he was far more at ease talking of abstract subjects — mathematics, finance, even art were safely impersonal enough for him to discuss at length without becoming even the least bit involved.

"Quite simply, I have no need for it, and therefore no desire for it. Most women marry simply in order to be supported and taken care of by a man. I can support and take care of myself, and I prefer to do so. Furthermore, the fortune that so many young women hope to marry into can be gone in an instant, you know." The defiant lift of her chin and the faintest trace of bitterness in her voice reminded him that something quite similar had happened to her in her life.

Again, the gaunt and haunted face of the previous Marquess of Shelburne flashed across Sebastian's mind. For someone as disciplined and ambitious as Cecilia to have seen her father, mentor, and teacher, consumed by the fever of gambling must have been disappointing to the extreme. And again, Sebastian felt the stab of guilt and despair at the role he had played in the Marquess's ruin.

"But what about love?" he heard himself asking.

"Love?" Cecilia stared at him as though he had just sprouted wings or grown another head.

"Yes, love." Sebastian could not help smiling at her patent astonishment. "Not everyone marries for a fortune. People do occasionally marry for love, you know."

"Love is for those who can find no other interest or passion in life. It is the merest excuse to feel strongly about something."

"I cannot agree with you. I feel sure that—"

But she was not to hear what he felt sure of, for at that precise moment Barbara and Neville, nearly overcome with laughter, returned from the floor.

"Did you ever see such a shocking quiz of a turban in your entire life?" Barbara gasped.

"No, never—except when she wore it last year. I thought I had never seen anything uglier then, but to try to disguise it with diamond aigrettes and plumes? It has only made an ugly thing uglier." Neville's eyes were dancing with suppressed laughter. "And yet she lords it over everyone as though she were the superior creature instead of an heiress with nothing to recommend her but her fortune, or a woman who confuses sparklers with style."

Barbara let out another delicious peal of laughter and Cecilia, watching the two of them, thought she had never seen Miss Wyatt so animated—or her brother either, for that matter.

"Your brother swears that you do not care for dancing,

Lady Cecilia, but you really must insist on his leading you to the floor just once. He is the very essence of grace, and he dances divinely." Barbara turned to her fiancé with a coquettish smile. "If only you would learn from him, Charrington, I am persuaded you would quite enjoy it. You must accompany me to my next sitting, and while I am being immortalized, you can learn the finer points of dancing."

The earl smiled indulgently at his fiancée. "Are you sure it is not because he enjoys dancing that Shelburne does it so well? I, as you often like to tell me, am an old sobersides, and therefore something as exuberant as dancing is quite foreign to my nature. Though I would be delighted for an excuse to attend your next sitting, I do not think that Shelburne, for all his skill, is likely to improve my dancing. And how does the portrait progress, Lady Cecilia?"

"For the amount of time she spends in her studio, it ought to be nearly finished by now." Neville scoffed. "She says she wishes to get the sketch absolutely perfect before she begins to apply the paint, but it is my belief that she works at it so she does not have to enjoy herself."

He turned to Barbara. "You must teach her something of that during your sittings, Miss Wyatt, for you are one of the few people whose portrait she has painted, besides Emily Cowper and Dorothea Lieven, who is not a bluestocking or dangerously close to it. You may call Charrington an old sobersides, but mark my words, he is nothing compared to Cecy. Why, she even pays the tradesmen's bills on time, if you can believe such a thing."

"But here"—Neville held out his arm to his sister—"I shall do as Miss Wyatt suggests and ask you to dance. No, don't glare at me, for I shan't take no for an answer. You had one of the best dancing masters in all of Italy, so I know you can dance."

Cecilia could hardly refuse without appearing churlish in front of the earl and his fiancée, so, with as good grace as she could muster, she allowed her brother to lead her onto the floor.

"Really, Neville, it is too bad of you. You know I don't care for it," she began crossly.

Her brother opened his blue eyes wide. "But why ever not? You are quite good at it, you know. And you cannot complain about your partner's lack of conversation, because you already know I have none, or at least not the sort you enjoy."

"You know that I enjoy conversation that is useful—the sort where I can learn something from someone."

"Like Charrington? No, don't poker up at me, Cecy, you look like an ape leader. There, that is better. Thank heavens it is a waltz and you will be forced to enjoy yourself." And clasping her hand in his, her brother glided them smoothly onto the floor.

"Actually, you and Charrington seemed to be having quite a pleasant conversation. It would do you good to smile more, the way you were then; it would wipe away that dreadful scowl you always wear."

"I don't scowl!"

"Don't you? Actually, I expect you don't consider it a scowl, just a frown of concentration—but let me tell you that the effect it has is the same, and it does your face no good. You will be wrinkled before your time."

"And I expect that vacuous expression that Miss Wyatt wears will keep her young."

"Well, it won't give her wrinkles, at any rate. Cut line, Cecy. I don't expect you to be like Miss Wyatt, but you don't have to be a dragon either. Where is the harm in taking a little pleasure in life?"

But Cecilia was too annoyed with her brother to reply, so they were silent for the rest of the dance as she struggled to think up an appropriately blistering retort. The more she thought, however, the more the music sounded in her ears and the more they whirled around the floor, faster and faster, until, by the time the dance ended, she couldn't remember what they had been arguing about.

"There, see, I knew you would enjoy yourself," Barbara

remarked as they rejoined her and Sebastian. "One cannot help it with someone like your brother. Yes"—she paused to eye Cecilia critically—"your complexion has definitely improved. Does she not look quite lovely, Charrington?"

"Quite. But then I have always thought Lady Cecilia to be quite lovely."

Chapter 13

Cecilia might have forgotten what she wished to say to her brother during their dance at Almack's, but she did not forget it the next morning when she received the haberdasher's bill. "Twenty cravats, Neville? But you just purchased a dozen of them from Beamon, Abbott, and Davison less than a month ago."

Neville laid down his fork. "There, I have told you not to look at bills at the breakfast table. It quite puts one off one's feed. Besides, you would not have your brother appearing in public with a soiled cravat, would you? Clean linen is the essential mark of a gentleman. Furthermore"—he leaned forward to look at her intently—"if you continue harping on such paltry topics, you will become a dead bore."

"Well, someone must, or we shall find ourselves in the poorhouse."

"If you applied yourself to finding a suitable husband with the same energy that you applied to your painting and your bill-paying, we should all be a good deal better off."

Cecilia ground her teeth. "Have care, Neville—it is portraits of people like Miss Wyatt that are keeping you in cravats. And while we are on the subject of Miss Wyatt, I should like to know what your intentions are in that direction."

Neville picked up his fork and knife and slowly, deliberately placed a slice of bacon topped with egg into his mouth, and chewed meditatively. He swallowed, and a slow smile spread across his handsome features. "Why, what do you mean, sister?"

"Only that I have never seen her so animated as she was last evening in your company. Have care what you are about, Neville. It is all very well for you to charm dashing young matrons or fashionable dowagers, but Miss Wyatt, who clearly yearns to make a name for herself in the *ton*, is not yet firmly enough established to risk the least whisper as to the nature of her reputation."

Her brother's blue eyes widened enormously. "And here I thought you considered such things to be a most trivial waste of one's energy."

"*I* do, but Miss Wyatt does not, and it is not fair of you to ... to ..."

"Relax, Cecy, I was only providing her with amusement for the evening, which is more than she gets from that old stick of a fiancé of hers. And if you were not fast becoming an old stick yourself, you would see that. Miss Wyatt is simply a person who likes to enjoy herself, and I tried, as any gentleman would, to do my level best to assist her in achieving her goal."

"Now." He rose. "I am off to enjoy myself, and I suggest that you do the same. You will never catch a husband if you continue to wear that Friday face of yours."

"And I tell you"— Cecilia also rose, clutching the pile of bills that had been delivered in the morning post—"that I have no intention of catching a husband."

"Have it your way, then, but if you had a husband, you would not have to spare a thought for those." And with an airy wave of his hand Neville indicated the sheaf of bills that she held, and then left her to fume silently.

Cecilia stalked off to her studio where she mixed pigments furiously for some time. Then, drawing a deep, steadying breath and slowly, deliberately picking up her brush, she began to apply the first daubs of paint to her portrait of Miss Wyatt.

Cecilia worked steadily to the point where she could do no more until the paint dried. Then, wiping her hands, she picked up her chalk and her half-filled sketchbook, flipped to a blank page, and began drawing feverishly, hoping against hope that sketching out her ideas for a possible large-scale painting of Cupid and Psyche would distract her from angry thoughts of Neville, her father, and the uncertainty of life after one's family had lost a fortune and one was forced to depend on the vagaries of public taste for one's livelihood.

When the idea for a painting of Cupid and Psyche had first come to her, Cecilia had been pleased with it—a young girl faced with insurmountable tasks that she accepted without complaint or self-pity—not to mention the god who loved her. But the more she sketched, the more dissatisfied she became with her product. No matter what she did or how hard she tried, Psyche remained looking downtrodden and submissive, while Cupid stayed stiff and godlike, rendering the entire scene lifeless and utterly devoid of passion or interest. In a fury of exasperation Cecilia flung the sketchbook across the studio.

"The Earl of Charrington," Tredlow announced as the sketchbook hit the opposite wall and fell with a flop to the floor.

"What do you want?" Cecilia whirled to glower at the intruder before her visitor's identity had fully penetrated her consciousness.

In her anger and frustration, she had still been carrying on an internal dialogue with her brother, and it was something of a shock to discover that it was not Neville, but Sebastian who stood regarding her quizzically from the doorway to her studio.

A chalk-covered hand rose to Cecilia's lips. "Oh no! I mean, I do beg your pardon." The hot flush of embarrassment flamed in her cheeks. It was the perfect disastrous end to a perfectly disastrous morning. At this moment, aside from wishing desperately that the earth would open up under her feet and swallow her without further delay, she wanted nothing more than to murder her brother.

"I take it that you have been having an altogether unsatisfactory morning. Is there any way I can help, or would you prefer to have me leave?" Recovering from his initial surprise, Sebastian strode into the room, stripping off his York tan gloves, for all the world as though he were preparing to do battle with her particular demons.

Cecilia could only stare at him. "What?"

"It looks to me as though you are having a rather bad time of it. Perhaps it would help you to talk about it. I am sure that you are quite capable of sorting things out for yourself, but there is nothing like talking about it to help get rid of the frustration so you can think clearly enough to solve the problem." Sebastian smiled at her look of utter astonishment. "At least that is the way it is with me. Problems, I can solve; it is my own annoyance that is more difficult to manage."

He had summed it up so accurately and exactly that Cecilia found herself overcome with the oddest feeling of gratitude for his wisdom and perspicacity. She could not ever remember having felt that way before. Her eyes stung with tears as unexpected as they were unwelcome. It was not like her to be such a watering pot. What was it about his few words of sympathy and a simple look of understanding that reduced her to this state of idiocy?

"My poor girl. What ever is it?" In two steps, he was across the room, hands on her shoulders, eyes dark with concern searching her face for some clue as to what was upsetting her.

The tears welled up, rolled over, and spilled down her cheeks before she even knew what was happening. Without a word, he pulled her gently into his arms.

It was too much. Waves of tension and exhaustion had been building inside her for weeks, and now they simply broke through their bounds. Helplessly she laid her cheek on his shoulder and struggled against the silent sobs that threatened to overwhelm her.

"Hush now. Tell me all about it, and perhaps we can think it through together." Gently, Sebastian stroked the blond curls that had pulled free from the coiled braid at the back of her head. "Now what is it that is troubling you so?"

With a heroic gulp, Cecilia pulled away angrily, ineffectively dashing at the tears on her cheeks.

Sebastian, who had endured what had felt like a lifetime of tears with his mother, not to mention every other female who had ever wanted something from him—money or marriage, or both—thought himself inured to female emotion by now. But these particular tears tore at his heart.

Pulling out a spotless handkerchief, he handed it to her and led her to the chair by the fireplace, taking the seat opposite her. "There now, dry your eyes and tell me everything."

The matter-of-fact tone had its effect, and Cecilia found herself calming down enough to speak. "It is nothing, really."

One skeptically raised eyebrow was ample proof that the Earl of Charrington was not a man to be put off by polite disclaimers.

"Well, it is this picture. I just cannot get it right, no matter what I do. You just happened to arrive at a particularly inopportune moment, as I was giving vent to quite unladylike feelings of frustration."

Sebastian did not think for a moment that something as simple as artistic frustration lay behind the look of exhaustion he read in her eyes, the tired slump of her shoulders. Tears in the eyes of a woman who greeted her patrons with the poise and aplomb that he had seen in few men were a clear indication that something more than frustration was at work here. No, if he had had to hazard a guess, Sebastian would venture to say that somehow that frippery brother of hers had something to do with her unhappy state of mind.

But he knew very well that Cecilia would never admit to
that.

So he stood up and walked over to retrieve the discarded
sketchbook. For some time he studied the unfinished sketch
in complete silence, then slowly flipped through the other
pages—Solomon deliberating over the child and its two
mothers, Dido building the citadel at Carthage, Hercules
slaying the Nemean Lion—examining them each in turn. At
last he appeared to reach a conclusion.

"What is it? What do you see?" Cecilia, who had been
watching his expression closely, could not help asking.

"I agree with you. Your latest sketch simply does not
measure up to the others. It lacks the power."

She waved her hand in a dismissive gesture of futility and
hopelessness.

A slow, almost tender smile spread across Sebastian's
face. "But it has nothing to do with your skill, or lack
thereof, as an artist. I would simply say the problem is that
you have never been in love."

"What?"

"Well, have you?" Sketchbook in hand, he walked back
to her chair, where he stood looking down at her with a mys-
terious smile on his lips and a disturbing light in his eyes.

"No! I mean, of course not!"

"Ah. I thought so."

For some reason that she simply could not fathom, Cecilia felt oddly defiant. "Well, have you?"

It was Sebastian's turn to be taken aback. He considered
it seriously for a moment. "No," he admitted slowly, "I don't
believe I have. But," he hastened to add, as he saw the tri-
umphant look creep into her eyes, "I *have* experienced passion . . . of *that sort* before, and I know what is lacking in
your drawing of Cupid and Psyche: it is their passion for one
another."

"See here." He turned to the sketch of Dido. "There is the
passion of determination in her stance, the heroic acceptance
of duty and danger in her eyes. And here"—he flipped to the

picture of Hercules—"here again are determination and
pride. All these are feelings that you as an artist—especially
a female artist trying to make a name as well as a living for
herself—must feel every day. Thus, you are able to capture
these passions in subtle ways because you understand them
so well—the clenched jaw here, the proud tilt of the head
there, the compressed lips here. But in these two"—he
pointed to Cupid and Psyche—"there is none of that."

Cecilia was artist enough to appreciate the truth in what
he said, and to be grateful to him for pointing it out to her,
unnerving though it was. But even more unnerving was the
surge of happiness that rose within her as she absorbed the
implications of his own admission. He did not love Barbara
Wyatt!

He had, however, admitted to feeling passion of *that sort*.

Cecilia looked up at him. What would it be like to experience passion with the Earl of Charrington? Her stomach
felt as though it had suddenly dropped to the floor, and her
heart thudded alarmingly. Her hands felt clammy and her
knees weak, as she remembered what it had felt like only
minutes before to be held in that reassuring embrace, to feel
the strength in his arms around her, the hardness of his chest
underneath her cheek, and the warmth of his hand on her
hair.

Sebastian watched with interest as color flooded Cecilia's cheeks. He saw comprehension dawn in her eyes as
her lips parted to speak, and he was seized with the most
desperate urge to pull her back into his arms and explore
those lips with his own, to inspire in her all the passion that
he knew lay within her, powerful, but untouched and un-
awakened.

"You are indeed clever, you know."

"What?" It was Sebastian's turn to look blank.

"You are quite right . . . about the picture, I mean. It *is*
lifeless. That is what was bothering me about it." Of course,
how she was going to remedy the situation was something

altogether different, and something Cecilia was not prepared even to contemplate.

"Perhaps I can help." Even as the words were leaving his mouth, Sebastian realized the full implication of what he was saying, but there was no way he could take it back now. He only wished that he really could help her experience the passion she needed to feel before she could attempt to capture the essence of subjects like Cupid and Psyche. "With your career, I mean."

He could not say why he had added the last sentence, but some devil in him wanted her to think about the implications of the previous sentence, to think about what it would be like to share passion with him—wanted her to long for him as he found himself longing for her.

"Thank you." It was all Cecilia could do to make her lips form the words. And then, desperate to break away from the intensity of his gaze, she reached up to take back her sketchbook.

The spell was broken. Sebastian slowly let out the breath he had been holding in. "I am having the house in Grosvenor Square redone and, until now, I had not given much thought to the decoration of the ballroom. At the moment it is rather dull; however, there is a medallion in the ceiling and there are panels between the pilasters that would be greatly enlivened with paintings. It occurs to me that there are just enough spaces, four on each side, in addition to the medallion, to hold pictures of the muses. It may not be history painting in quite the spirit you had envisioned, but it would be a beginning at least.

"In fact," he added, warming to his theme, "I envision Terpsichore in the medallion as the centerpiece with the other muses on the walls below her, surrounding her." He looked at Cecilia questioningly.

"Ah, er, I do not know what to say. Such a commission is very flattering, of course, but very expensive. I cannot accept a favor of such magnitude simply because you are a friend who wishes to help me."

Sebastian shook his head smiling. "Always the artist of rigorous principles. I am not asking you because you are a friend. I am asking you because you are C. A. Manners, the painter whose pictures I admired at the Royal Academy exhibition—pictures I admired so much that I became your patron first and your friend second."

He turned and walked over to examine Barbara's unfinished portrait. "And thus far, I am extremely pleased with the work that you have done for me. You have captured the spirit well, I think. Please say that you will at least consider my offer."

When he put it like that, he made it easy for her to accept, even though she still suspected that he was offering it out of kindness to her, rather than a real need to embellish his ballroom. "Very well, I shall think about it."

"Excellent. I suggest you meet me there at your earliest convenience—tomorrow, if you like—so that you can see what the project entails."

"Thank you." She smiled shyly. "I should like that."

And it was not until Sebastian was at the very door of her studio that he remembered why he had come. "Good heavens, I almost forgot again. Here is Sir Humphry Davy's paper on pigments that I promised you, along with a few observations of my own. Perhaps you might look it over, and then I could explain my thoughts to you."

Suddenly awkward, as though he had presumed too much on her time, Sebastian thrust the pages into her hand, bowed, and was gone, leaving Cecilia to gaze thoughtfully after him.

Chapter 14

The door closed behind him, and with a sigh of relief, Cecilia went back to her work. But her mind refused to focus. Her eyes kept drifting back to the rough sketch of Cupid and Psyche, and she kept hearing a deep voice saying *I would simply say that you have never been in love.*

No, she never had been in love before. She had been too busy with her career, and she had had no time for love—or anything else, for that matter. Nor had she had the inclination. Love, men, marriage, were all distractions from her ultimate goal of becoming an artist. It was this very single-mindedness that had allowed her to accomplish as much as she had managed to accomplish in a relatively short space of time. And she was proud of what she had accomplished.

It was only now, for the very first time in her life that she asked herself if perhaps she had missed something along the way—closeness, intimacy, the sharing of life with another person.

Cecilia had always been surrounded by friends and colleagues—artists, musicians, writers—people whose interests were as wide-ranging and insatiable as her own. But though they had exchanged thoughts and ideas, and explored new ways of looking at things, they had never truly shared anything, and she had never truly been close to anyone.

She had never looked into anyone else's eyes and seen what she had seen in Sebastian's—sympathy, concern, the reflection of her soul in his. And she had certainly never wondered what it would be like to be held in someone's arms, to feel someone's lips on hers, someone's hand caressing her.

Cecilia looked back at the picture of Cupid and Psyche. Even now, after the brief interlude when Sebastian had held her in his arms, stroked her hair, and comforted her in her distress, she could see what was wrong about her picture— what was lacking in it that made it seem so wooden and lifeless.

Seizing her chalk, she rubbed away some of the stiffer lines and made them more fluid, more pliable, thinking all the while as she did so of the feeling of flesh against flesh, the peculiar electric current that had seemed to flow between them wherever their bodies had touched one another, the strange hunger that had made her long for more, and regret that she had pulled away so quickly. And as the chalk moved slowly up to the faces of the lovers, she recalled the warm light in Sebastian's eyes as he had looked at her. Her fingers suddenly seemed to have a life of their own as the retraced lips and eyebrows, the tender curve of the cheek, the glow in the eyes.

At last the fever that had gripped her broke, and she awoke from her trancelike state. Hardly daring to do so, she studied her drawing again. Yes! That was it! Not completely, perhaps, but she had begun to capture the essence of what she had been striving for in the drawing from the very beginning.

How had the Earl of Charrington understood all this? And even more unnerving, how had he been able to make her see it?

Cecilia resolutely thrust such dangerous questions from her mind. The point was that she *had* been able to improve her picture, and this revelation was going to improve her as an artist. How it would affect the rest of her life was utterly immaterial.

In the meantime, she had a large commission to look forward to—one that did not involve a portrait, but gave her the opportunity she craved to give her imagination full rein. It was time to put aside all thoughts of Cupid and Psyche and come up with ideas for her nine paintings of the muses, so that she would have at least some rough sketches to submit for the Earl's approval when she met him in Grosvenor Square the next day. She might suspect that the Earl of Charrington was offering her this opportunity out of kindness and friendship, but that did not mean she was not going to respond to this offer in the most professional way possible.

The next day—having sent a footman with a note to Curzon Street, establishing a time for their meeting in Grosvenor Square—Cecilia dressed with more care than usual for her meeting with the Earl of Charrington, as she tried to present her most professional appearance. Her walking dress of French gray Circassian cloth was simple though elegantly cut, and devoid of any trimming except for bands of white lutestring at the hem. Even the severe cut of her bonnet of slate-colored silk more closely resembled a gentleman's hat than the more extravagantly trimmed headgear of those who aspired to the highest kick of fashion.

But for all its businesslike air, her costume was extremely becoming, the soft gray highlighting the gold of her hair and the delicacy of her complexion, which, by the time she had completed her vigorous walk to Grosvenor Square, was glowing with her exertion and her pleasure in the fineness of the day.

Cecilia had been so occupied with her work for the past several weeks that she had barely stepped outside, and now she took great delight in the softness of the air, with its promise of spring, and the bright blue of the sky, broken here and there by fluffy white clouds.

The Earl of Charrington's house in Grosvenor Square

was an imposing mansion, with such an impressively wide façade that it made Cecilia think it had once been two houses now cleverly combined into one. It was filled with workmen—plasterers, painters, and carpenters—busily putting on the finishing touches throughout the building. A footman, who had been stationed at the door, opened it and led her up the broad marble staircase to the first-floor drawing room where the earl, bent over a table covered with plans, was busily conferring with a serious-looking gentleman.

At the sound of footsteps, he looked up. "Ah, Lady Cecilia." Sebastian's face lit up when he saw her. Excusing himself, he hurried over to greet her. "I am delighted that you could come today."

It had only been yesterday that she had seen him, only one day since he had proposed his plan to her, yet the welcome in his smile and the warmth in his eyes made Cecilia feel as though she were returning home after a long journey. It had been years since anyone had made her feel that way. Not since Naples, when she had come home after a long day of sketching antiquities in Pompeii or copying masterpieces in the queen's fine collection of paintings to have her father smile eagerly and hold out a hand for her sketchbook, had she felt that her presence was looked forward to.

"Mr. Wilkins here has come to consult with me about the design for the main reception rooms. Miss Wyatt, who knows a great deal about such things, has assured me that an anteroom and two drawing rooms on the first floor are quite sufficient, such that this third drawing room at the back simply must be turned into a ballroom that will rival any ballroom to be found in London."

Sebastian had been walking as he was talking and he now ushered her into a magnificent room whose vaulted ceiling was decorated with exquisite plasterwork. "As you see, the space is beautifully proportioned, but it lacks color and warmth, without which—to my mind, at least—it remains dull and formidable. Formality is all very well in the main reception rooms, but it seems to me that if a room has been created for the purpose of dancing, then it should make one feel like dancing. Hence my idea for the paintings I proposed to you. But I see you have brought your sketchbook with you. Excellent."

Cecilia walked over to a small side table that still remained in the empty room and opened her sketchbook. "They are very rudimentary, of course, for I had not seen the room itself, but I took the liberty of making some preliminary drawings."

She held her breath as the earl leaned over to examine the sketches. He was so close that his shoulder touched hers, and she could see the muscles in his cheek tighten as he flipped silently from one drawing to the next, pausing every now and then to consider it carefully, then flipping back to the previous sketch and on to the next.

At last he turned toward her and smiled. "Perfect. Just what I had hoped for. They all capture a sense of lightness and grace. And Terpsichore, especially, as the center of them all makes one feel that one cannot help but dance. . . . May I?" He bowed and held out his hand to her.

And so, as if it were the most natural thing in the world, she took his hand and allowed him to swing her onto the floor in a silent waltz. Her first thought as they swirled around the room was that Barbara was wrong; he was a superb dancer, with all the grace, the strength, and the rhythm of a natural-born athlete.

Her second thought was that Barbara, if she ever took the time to recognize her fiancé's skill, would enjoy a lifetime of waltzes with him under Cecilia's painting of Terpsichore. This thought made her feel as though someone had just opened up a window in the middle of winter and let in a blast of cold air.

But then Sebastian's hold tightened on her and he smiled down at her conspiratorially, warming her, making her feel once again as though she were specially welcome there. "If I had not been assured repeatedly by your brother that the case is otherwise, I would say that you loved to dance, Lady

Cecilia. You are as light and graceful as Terpsichore herself."

With you I am. Only with you, she could not help thinking. "Perhaps that is because there is no one else around." Cecilia felt her face grow hot as she realized the full implication of her words. "I mean that with no one else around, it is purely movement—dancing and nothing else—no social competition, no indication to the world at large where one stands in the hierarchy of the *ton* according to one's choice of partner."

"Ah." He looked down at her, his dark eyes unfathomable, but she felt as though he could see into her very soul, and knew that she reveled in the way they moved together as easily as if they were one. She longed for him to hold her closer, so she could feel the strength and reassurance of him as she felt the strength and reassurance of his understanding and appreciation. What would it be like to be the wife of a man such as this? To finish an evening of dancing secure in the prospect of retiring to the intimacy of one's own private rooms to share . . .

Cecilia's cheeks grew hotter. She could not believe she was thinking such thoughts—she who had always been too busy for men and marriage. How could she be feeling something so perilously close to envy toward a woman whose insipidity and superficial values she despised?

"So you think it a project that could interest you, then?"

Cecilia gulped and brought herself back to the present—to the comfortably reassuring world of the professional artist. "Oh yes. Most definitely. And indeed, I am most grateful to you for thinking of me."

"No need for gratitude, Lady Cecilia. The pictures you showed tell me that I will be getting the very best for my ballroom. As someone who strives for the very best in all that I do, I am both pleased and relieved to have found someone of your skill and talent to realize my vision. However, there is one more request that I would make."

"Yes?" Cecilia could not imagine why—with artists, architects, and builders at his command, all eager to do his bidding and to gratify his slightest whim in the decoration of a truly impressive mansion—the earl should sound so tentative. Here was a man with a fortune at his disposal, not to mention a title and a formidable reputation, who suddenly seemed remarkably unsure of himself. What was it that he wished to ask of her?

"I should like . . . I mean, I wonder if you could see your way to using this particular face as the face of Terpsichore." He walked over to an alcove where he retrieved a small oval picture wrapped in Holland cloth that had been propped up against the wall. "It is a picture I have treasured for some time now, since I found it in a print shop in the Strand some years ago. It caught my eye then as the picture of someone I would like to know—someone who possessed both intelligence and character, but someone who could still laugh at the absurdities of the world. I like to think that the Greek deities were very much like this girl: inspired, yet human."

He unwrapped the picture and turned it around so she could see it.

Cecilia gasped and gripped the table for strength and support as the world spun around her. She felt hot, then cold, and slightly dizzy all at once.

"I beg your pardon." Sebastian took her firmly by the shoulders and led her to an abandoned chair in the corner of the room and tenderly helped her into it. "I had no idea it would affect you this way."

"Whe . . . where did you say you got this?" Cecilia clutched the arms of the chair in the vain hope that it would stop the world from spinning.

"In a print shop in the Strand. The proprietor said he usually sold only prints—etchings and engravings—but the gentleman who sold it to him was so desp . . . er, insistent, that he made an exception, and—"

"How dared he!" Entirely forgetting her surroundings, or her previous weakness, Cecilia leapt up and began pacing the room.

"I *gave* it to him. I *gave* it to Papa. I would *never* sell such a thing. It was but a childish piece of art, done when I was only twelve years old. How could he have sold it! Put it in a shop window for all the world to see! The wretch! Oh what am I do? How could he? How could he?"

Then, utterly exhausted by her outburst, she sank back into the chair again and buried her face in her hands.

"Cecilia, my poor girl. Please do not take on so." Heedless of the dust and his spotless biscuit-colored pantaloons, Sebastian knelt on the floor in front of her and took her hands in his.

"It has *not* been in a shop window all these years, but in my library, as a treasured possession, and an inspiration to me for all the time I have owned it. Please do not distress yourself so. I beg you."

Gently he drew her hands away from her face, forcing her to look up at him. "The owner of the shop swore to me that he had only just received it the day before, and that he would never have purchased it if he had not thought it excellently done."

"But how could he have sold it?" Her eyes were bright with unshed tears and her lips trembled so much she could barely form the words.

His heart ached for her. In truth, it *was* like selling your child to give its portrait over to a print seller, and Sebastian had played no small part in that sale. What was he to do? How ever was he going to make it up to her?

"Listen to me." He gathered her hands into his. "I do not know precisely how or why that picture got into the shop, but believe me, since it came into my possession, it has had the tenderest care and concern lavished upon it that anyone could wish. That face has been my constant and closest companion since the moment I brought it home. It has been my strength and inspiration, the friend I never had but always longed for, my ideal person, my ideal woman—which is why I want that image immortalized in my ballroom.

"Cecilia, please believe me. I never meant to distress

you." He smiled a crooked smile. "I suppose that, in essence, what I want to say is that you have always been my muse, whether you knew it or not. And I want you to continue to be my muse, enshrined forever in this ballroom."

Too overwhelmed by it all, Cecilia pulled her hands away. "I . . . I must think about it. It has been rather a shock to me. I cannot—I mean, I must have some time to think it over."

"Of course. Take all the time that you wish. I understand, and I apologize most sincerely for upsetting you. I suppose I should never have shown it to you, but somehow, after I realized that my girl in the portrait was also C. A. Manners, the artist whose pictures I so admired, it seemed the height of dishonesty not to tell you that I had that picture. The only question was how."

"I thank you for telling me, but now, if you will excuse me, I must go."

Cecilia rose and, clutching her sketchbook to her like a talisman, she hurried out of the room, down the stairs, and into the street where she paused to gulp deep, steadying breaths of fresh air in a desperate attempt to regain her composure. Then, chin held high, she marched off in the direction of Golden Square.

Chapter 15

By the time Cecilia reached her studio she had calmed herself to some degree—enough, at least to tell herself that in spite of Sebastian being the owner of her self-portrait, he had had no part in its sale. That had been solely her father's doing. As such, she relegated this new betrayal on his part with the other betrayals and failures he had committed after they had left Italy and returned to London: the money he had lost, the nights he hadn't come home, his utter lack of interest in anything but the gaming table. In short, the slow disintegration of a once vital and loving man. All this she had done her best to forgive or ignore until that last rainy night when he had struggled home, soaked to the bone, and nearly dead with the cold and the wet.

Cecilia would not let herself think of those days because the anger and frustration would have destroyed her or turned her into a bitter woman, old before her time. She preferred instead to bury the unhappy memories and recall only the happier ones of warm, sunny days spent in the villa overlooking the Bay of Naples.

So once again, as she had done so many times before, she put all thoughts of this particular betrayal out of her head and began to work on Barbara's portrait, so that it would be ready when the subject herself arrived. Barbara was due to come for a final sitting that day and Cecilia wanted the painting to be as complete as possible, so that she could concentrate on the areas that presented the biggest problems.

As always, her work exerted a calming influence on Cecilia, and as she mixed colors, added a touch here, a stroke there, stepping back from time to time in order to assess the effect, her mind emptied itself of all thoughts of her father, until she could think of nothing but the work before her.

She applied a finishing touch and stopped to look at the portrait as a whole, and then a host of questions and thoughts of Grosvenor Square came flooding back with a vengeance.

Where would Barbara's portrait hang in the mansion? Would it be at the head of the grand staircase, or over the mantel in the drawing room, or even in the ballroom? Would it take the place of her own self-portrait in Sebastian's mind? Would Barbara now become his ideal woman and his constant companion? She would be his wife in spite of the earl's admission that he too had never been in love before. Was it just possible that being in constant contact with a beautiful woman day after day, no matter how divergent their interests or how ill-suited they were to one another, might lead to a tenderer regard, and the sort of intimacy that came after years of living together and sharing one another's lives, no matter how tangentially?

Would he look into Barbara's eyes the way he had looked into hers, making her feel unique in all the world, as though she were the only woman that existed for him? Surely not. Surely theirs was simply a marriage of convenience. Barbara had admitted as much on her part, but what of Sebastian? He was a man of principles and ideals. He had no need to marry anyone, so why had he chosen Barbara Wyatt? Was it purely out of respect and gratitude to her father, the man who had helped him get his start, or was it something deeper?

Cecilia did not know which answer she wished for. On the one hand, she wanted to believe that Sebastian was a man of honor who would not marry a woman for whom he cared nothing. On the other hand, she very much did not want him to care about Barbara Wyatt. She did know one thing, however; first, if she was going to be working on pictures for the Earl of Charrington's ballroom day after day, she was going to have to find a way of putting the Earl of Charrington himself out of her mind; and the sooner she was able to do that by finishing both the portrait of Barbara and the paintings for the ballroom, the better.

And the best way to complete her project was to start on it now. Cecilia picked up her sketchbook and began filling in the rough conceptualizations for her drawings of the muses. Once she had completed those, she could take exact measurements for the panels, order the canvas and the stretchers, and begin work in earnest.

Her professional interest eventually reasserted itself, and Cecilia lost all concept of time until Tredlow came to announce, "Miss Wyatt to see you, my lady."

The beauty looked more ravishing than ever. There was a sparkle in her eye, an animation in her expression and in her voice as she greeted her portrait painter, that Cecilia could not remember ever having seen or heard.

She was about to ascribe it to the near completion of the portrait or the fineness of the day when she heard footsteps in the hall, and saw Neville's blond head pop around the corner of the doorway.

"Cecy, I was just . . . oh, Miss Wyatt." He executed a well-feigned start and sauntered casually into the studio. "How fortunate that I happened in at this particular moment. I wanted to thank you again for standing up with me at Almack's, and to ask you to promise me another dance next time. You did assure me that I could count on your presence there every Wednesday evening, did you not?"

"But of course, my lord. I would not dream of being anywhere else. But it is *I* who am indebted to *you*. No woman could hope to have a more graceful partner than you, nor one whose taste is so much admired. I must say that I was

quite overwhelmed with requests for dances after being led
to the floor by you. It is clear that the Marquess of Shelburne
is a leader in the *ton,* and that those who aspire to any sort
of fashion are quick to follow his lead."

"Only in the cut of his coats and the tying of his cravat, I
am afraid, dear lady." Neville sighed dramatically, and
solemnly laid a hand over his heart. "Until now he has con
fined his fastidious taste to the commissioning of mere articles of tailoring, and it has been said that he would never
find a human being worthy of admiration, his standards
being so impossibly high. But at last the utterly exquisite,
the incomparable Miss Wyatt appeared on the scene, and he
is able to lay his admiring heart at her feet."

His tone was reverent, but the blue eyes were dancing
with amusement, and Barbara broke into a delicious peal of
laughter. "You are absurd, my lord, and far too kind. You
make me feel like some highly finished work of art that
should be placed in a museum. I am not so stiff and formal
as all that. I need gaiety surrounding me. I need dancing, and
music, and laughter, and throngs of elegant, fashionable
people."

"And so you shall have it. Believe me, Miss Wyatt, dancing at Almack's is only the beginning. You will soon have
the *ton* at your feet, and you will be so sought after that you
will be longing for a moment's peace and solitude. And I,
poor fellow, shall have to fight my way through crowds of
admirers simply to catch a glimpse of you. A dance with you
will soon be quite beyond the reach of all but the most per-
sistent of mortals, and the print shops will be filled with engravings of your picture, if Cecy will ever finish it." He cast
a teasing glance in his sister's direction.

"Which she would do if her brother were not distracting
her model to such a degree," Cecilia retorted, a suspicious
glint in her eye.

"I beg your pardon. I interrupt serious business, and
worse yet, I make Miss Wyatt laugh. One cannot be immortalized for posterity if one is laughing; it is simply not

done." Neville pulled a ludicrously serious face which only had the effect of making Barbara laugh all the harder.

"There. I have done it again," he declared with great satisfaction. "I have proven that I am, as my sister constantly complains, a useless good-for-nothing; therefore I shall spare you my disturbing company and take myself off to Tattersall's. They say Crompton is selling up, and no one knows a prime bit of blood better than Crompton. There is bound to be something worth seeing. Fortunately, I am in desperate need of a new hack, and nothing is so gratifying as doing a friend a good turn. Do you drive in the park, Miss Wyatt?"

Barbara nodded, her eyes sparkling.

"Good. Then perhaps I shall see you there. I assure you that my taste in horseflesh is as exquisite as my taste in cravats and coats."

A quick graceful bow and he was gone as unexpectedly as he had come, leaving one of the occupants of the room, at least, with an appreciative smile on her face.

"Is your brother always this amusing, Lady Cecilia?" Barbara asked.

"Sometimes," Cecilia admitted honestly. Neville was utterly unreliable, a spendthrift who could never be counted upon for anything except landing them in dun territory, but there was no denying the infectiousness of his optimism, or his enthusiasm for a life of pleasure and self-indulgence. "Yes, he can be quite amusing when he wishes to be."

"You are fortunate indeed." Barbara sighed. "My papa is never amusing. He and Charrington think of nothing but business and money. I find it insufferably tedious."

"It certainly is if one does not have them." Cecilia bit her tongue, but the words were already out of her mouth. What ever had possessed her to speak so sharply? She sounded like a vulgar fishwife.

"I shall just have to see to it that Charrington learns to live more like a gentleman—more like your brother." Barbara continued as though Cecilia had never spoken. "When

I become mistress of Charrington House, I shall have so many routs and balls that he will not have time for anything else."

A vision of the beautiful ballroom in Grosvenor Square rose before Cecilia's eyes, and once again she felt the warm touch of Sebastian's hand and saw the smile in his eyes. Would he smile into Barbara's eyes the way he had smiled into hers as they whirled around the floor? Or would he glance up at the ceiling to see Terpsichore smiling down at him with Cecilia's face—the face that he claimed to be that of his ideal woman, his ideal companion?

No, Cecilia told herself firmly. She was simply a model for his ideal, not the real thing. She would never be the real thing, never experience the unsettling feelings that had threatened to overwhelm her when she was in Sebastian's arms, the longing and the hunger for she knew not quite what—the excruciating awareness of every sense in her body. No, madness lay with thoughts like that, and she was not that sort of person. Long ago, she had consciously chosen to ignore that part of life—the part between men and women—and dedicate herself instead to her art. One could not be a true professional and give in to such distractions as those.

But, a tiny voice in her head insisted, *you gave up that part of your life before you even knew what you were giving up. If you had felt then what you felt with him in the ballroom, would you have found it so easy to give up? Would you have traded being in the arms of a man who admires and understands you so easily for brushes and paints if you had been in his arms before you did so?*

". . . shall have to ask your brother what he considers to be the best taste in frames and settings . . ." Barbara's voice broke into Cecilia's uncomfortable reverie.

"Ask Neville? Why not ask Char—er, your fiancé?"

"Charrington?" Barbara looked at Cecilia, her eyes wide with astonishment. "Ask Charrington? What could he possibly know about such a thing?"

"He seems to understand a good deal about art. And since the portrait was his idea, I should think him extremely qualified to advise you."

"Charrington? *My* Charrington? Why, he only knows the price of canal shares; he has not the least idea of taste or fashion," his fiancée responded, forgetting entirely that it had been *her* Charrington's visit to the exhibition at the Royal Academy that had been responsible for her introduction to Lady Cecilia in the first place.

My Charrington. Cecilia struggled to ignore the unworthy stab of envy these casually uttered words produced, but, try as she would, she could not. *And you had better not ignore it,* she admonished herself. *You had better not forget that for all his kindness to you, he is* her Charrington, *and she is soon to become his countess—a fact that you would do well to remember.*

Chapter 16

In fact, Barbara's Charrington had spent more of his time thinking about art, and one artist in particular, than he had about anything else for several days after Cecilia's visit to Grosvenor Square. First and foremost, he was concerned with her distress over the discovery of her self-portrait in his possession. How could he have been such an insensitive fool as to spring it on her in that way? But the more he considered it, the more he realized that there had been no good way to tell her that he was in possession of that picture, sold by her father in an effort to pay his gambling debts.

Sebastian's conscience would not let him keep her in the dark. As a matter of fact, his conscience was being damnably difficult about his own personal role in those gambling debts, but at the moment, he did not have the courage to tell her about that.

Someday he would explain how he had come to play so often against the Marquess of Shelburne—how he had seen his own father in the haunted eyes of the desperate peer, and punished him for succumbing to the grip of the same obsession that had destroyed his father, his mother, and a good deal of his own life as well. But it would require a good deal of explanation, and he was not sure enough of her yet.

Sebastian desperately hoped that Cecilia felt as close to

him as he did to her—hoped that she recognized the special affinity that existed between them whenever they fell into conversation—an affinity so intense that words barely had to be uttered for the other one to understand. But he was not sure. As a man of science, he knew the dangers of wishing so strongly for a thing to be true that one unconsciously arranged the evidence to prove it so. He had tried to remain rational and objective, to tell himself that the closeness he felt to her was truly reflected in her eyes and her smile—that it was not just the product of his imagination built up over the years of living with her portrait.

Sebastian glanced over at the portrait now. The hazel eyes still seemed to look straight at him with curious interest. The mouth, with its shy smile, still invited conversation, and the faintly raised eyebrows still promised the ironic, half-skeptical view of life that the real Cecilia espoused so strongly. And where was his portrait going to live now?

He had not really stopped to consider this question. Until he had discovered that C. A. Manners, Lady Cecilia, and the girl in the portrait were one in the same, it had not really much mattered where he hung his picture. He had planned to move it from the library on Curzon Street to the library of the house in Grosvenor Square, where it would keep him company as it always had. Now, however, everything had changed.

He was reasonably certain that Barbara did not give a rap for him as long as he was a peer of ancient lineage who was willing to keep her in the style to which she was accustomed and to give her the entrée to the *ton* that she craved. He was also reasonably certain that she would take great exception to having a self-portrait of the woman who had painted her own portrait gracing her husband's library.

There was only one answer to this dilemma, and that was to return the picture to its rightful owner: its creator. In some measure, it would repay her for her father's original betrayal, and, at the same time, it would assure her as to the picture's continued privacy and protection.

But then he would be left with nothing, in a house that was not truly his own.

While it was true that Sebastian owned the house in Grosvenor Square, he had only just recently acquired it, and he had acquired it with Barbara in mind. It was just the sort of house that a woman who wanted to make a name for herself in society could flaunt before the beau monde, a house where she could entertain on a scale lavish enough to ensure her a place in the *ton*. It was not the sort of house in which Sebastian felt at home. And now he was about to rid himself of one of the few things that would have made it feel like home.

Yet he had shied away from admitting to Cecilia that the mansion in Grosvenor Square had only recently become his. Why was that? He suspected that it had to do with his relationship with Cecilia. Though he had not precisely deceived her, he had been eager for her to think that the house in Grosvenor Square was the family town house—lost to creditors, perhaps, and in need of repair and redecorating, but something that had been part of his birthright—not something that he had just acquired to gratify the social ambitions of his wife-to-be.

Why had he allowed her to think that? Why had he avoided all discussion of the mansion's background and provenance? Sebastian could not say precisely why it was, except that redecorating one's own house to suit a prospective wife's taste was a great deal different from acquiring one just for her. That was not the gesture of a man who was making a marriage of convenience. And the more he came to know Cecilia, the more Sebastian wanted her to understand that his marriage to Miss Wyatt was precisely that.

Having decided on a course of action as far as Cecilia's self-portrait was concerned, Sebastian's first inclination was to seize the excuse to see her again, and deliver it immediately to Golden Square, thus reassuring himself that she would still see him.

When she had left Grosvenor Square that day, fighting

back tears of shock and outrage, he had not been at all sure that she would want to see him ever again. And while it was true that she had thanked him in a way for giving her self-portrait a home after her father had so carelessly disposed of it, she had not been best pleased that he had kept its existence a secret from her once he had become aware of her identity.

Should he take it to her and risk her displeasure by intruding on her privacy, or should he simply have it delivered, and hope against hope that she would feel compelled to see him and thank him for giving it to her?

But Sebastian had reckoned without Cecilia's dedication to her profession; several days later, when he went once again to confer on the drawings Mr. Wilkins had prepared for the Grosvenor Square house, he was astounded to discover Cecilia there, engaged in a lively discussion with Mr. Wilkins himself.

For a moment, Sebastian paused on the threshold of the ballroom, envying them and their easy conversation about position and perspective—the obvious sharing of professional experience and opinions, as well as the clear respect they held for one another's skills and talents.

Then, as if she sensed his presence, Cecilia turned around and greeted him. "My lord, I had not expected to see you here today. I have just come to confer with Mr. Wilkins regarding the precise dimensions and exact positions for the panels, and he has most graciously offered to have them measured for me so I may order the canvas."

Her voice was crisply professional, her manner businesslike, but just for a moment, when he had first entered the ballroom, Sebastian thought he had seen a smile of welcome in her eyes. Or had he wanted to see it so much that he had simply imagined it?

He longed to recapture those moments in the ballroom when he had held her in his arms and whirled her around the floor. There had been a smile on her face, a glow in her eyes as though she were truly enjoying herself. And he was the one with whom she had enjoyed herself.

But now, oddly enough, he was purely and simply proud of her—proud of her professional attitude toward her work, proud that, ignoring the upsetting circumstances of the last time she had left Grosvenor Square, she was continuing with the project she had agreed to do. "Of course, Lady Cecilia. I beg your pardon for interrupting. If there is any way in which Mr. Wilkins or the workmen or I can assist you, please do not hesitate to let me know."

Lord, he sounded like an old stiff-rump, but his delight at seeing her there had taken him quite by surprise, and it made him as awkward as a schoolboy. "Forgive me for not offering before—I mean, I am not well versed in these things—but you must tell me what you require to work here. We shall create a studio for you exactly as you wish it to be."

"Oh no. I can easily do the work in my own studio." Cecilia began before she realized that she could not easily accommodate canvases the size that would be required for the ballroom. But the idea of working there day after day in a room where he and his wife-to-be would be entertaining all of London was something she was not ready to contemplate.

"As you will. I was only thinking of what would be most convenient for you, and—"

"I appreciate that, and indeed, I thank you for it"—she interrupted him hastily—"but truly there is no need."

"And it would give me great pleasure to think of you working here in my house," he finished softly, so softly that only she, who was standing closer to him than the architect, could hear.

Spots of pink glowed in her cheeks, and she hastily lowered her eyes to the pad of paper on which she had been writing measurements.

So she was not indifferent to him, he thought triumphantly. Then, taking pity on her, he excused himself. "Forgive me. I intrude upon your work. I shall just take a look in the drawing room and then be on my way."

Lady Cecilia hastily replaced her expression with the coolly businesslike appearance she assumed with most of her patrons, but the ice had been broken, and the awkwardness of the initial encounter after the revelations concerning her self-portrait had disappeared. Sebastian now felt free to call on her in Golden Square, to return her picture to its rightful home.

Selecting a day and time when he knew there was to be an auction at Tattersall's that no admirer of horseflesh would miss, Sebastian appeared at Golden Square with the heavily wrapped picture under his arm.

This time when Tredlow announced him, Lady Cecilia truly did seem glad, but — as she launched immediately into a discussion of her plans for the panels with the muses — Sebastian realized, with a lowering feeling, that it was excitement over the project, and not his arrival, that was responsible for the welcoming smile on her face.

"See here." Cecilia opened to a sketch of Polyhymnia. I know that it is only pictures of the muses and not a history painting, but I have taken the opportunity to suggest the heroic and the ideal in all of my presentations, by including in the background various scenes from mythology that exemplify the power the arts hold over us — their power to ennoble us and inspire us, to overcome our selfish natures and our aimless lives. Not," she added with a rueful smile, "that anyone dancing in your ballroom will either notice or care about being ennobled or inspired."

"Perhaps not." Sebastian smiled in return. "But I know I shall. As you know, I do my best to avoid dancing, and therefore I am constantly in search of distraction at these wretched affairs."

Again there was the conspiratorial twinkle in his eyes that made her feel that he and she alone in all of London knew what it was like to be bored at a ball. Cecilia could not help chuckling. "Well, if I can provide even a moment's diversion for you, then I shall consider my paintings a success."

So he was not particularly looking forward to leading the future Countess of Charrington onto the floor. The thought should not have brought such immense satisfaction to Cecilia, but it did.

Sebastian watched the variety of expressions flit across her face, from eagerness to amusement, to something else that looked remarkably like a flush of self-consciousness— a self-consciousness he wished desperately he could interpret, but it was gone as quickly as it had appeared.

"It was not, however, to ask you about your plans for the ballroom paintings that I am calling on you, but to give you this. If you will have it." Awkwardly he thrust the bulky package toward her.

Mystified both by the package and his abruptness, Cecilia struggled to untie the string and undo the wrappings. "Oh my!"

"I felt it was high time it was returned to its rightful owner, and restored to its original surroundings."

"But you paid for it. I mean, I couldn't accept—"

"Why ever not? Not only were you its original owner, you were also its subject and its creator—and a very youthful creator at that. I hope that, in some way, having it with you in your studio will bring back some of those memories of happier times that you were so good as to share with me."

"You are far too kind," she whispered as tears stung her eyelids. "How can I ever thank you? You are always looking out for me, it seems—though until I met you I was under the impression that I was doing a rather good job of it myself."

"You can thank me by continuing to let me look out for you." Sebastian replied softly. Then, afraid that her independent spirit might balk at such a notion, he raised her hand to his lips and was gone.

It was not until the door shut behind him that Cecilia realized that she infinitely preferred having her picture remain where it had been all this time: in his library, keeping him company.

Chapter 17

Companionship was very much the topic of conversation the next morning at the breakfast table in Golden Square, as Cecilia, wiping the last few crumbs of toast from her fingers, rang for the footman and handed him a hastily scrawled note. "Please deliver this to Miss Wyatt and wait for an answer, Sedley. Thank you."

"Don't bother to send Sedley. He can be better employed picking up the new waistcoat I ordered. I shall convey whatever message you have for Miss Wyatt," Neville offered as he polished off his rasher of bacon.

His sister eyed him with considerable astonishment.

"I am escorting Miss Wyatt and her great-aunt to see Napoleon's carriage and all the other entertaining sights to be found at the Egyptian Hall."

"The Egyptian Hall!"

"Just because you consider specimens of cameoleopards, elephants, and rhinoceri to be unworthy of your notice does not mean that everyone does."

"I suppose so," his sister responded doubtfully. "But I would have thought that Miss Wyatt's fiancé would already have introduced her to the delights of the place."

Neville snorted. "What? Charrington? He is as high in the instep as you are where amusements are concerned, which is to say that nothing seems to amuse him. Besides, he is too busy in the City to escort her there or to a concert in the Argyll Rooms, which she has also never seen. Even *you* will admit that they are worth a visit."

"With you, Neville? To what purpose?"

"What do you mean, *to what purpose?* Why does there have to be a purpose to everything? For the sheer fun of it. Little though you may appreciate it, Cecy, I am highly sought after as an escort. I always look the fashionable gentleman—complete to a shade, if I do say so myself. And I am thought to be a most entertaining companion."

"That is just what I am afraid of. Have care, Neville. Miss Wyatt may be the Earl of Charrington's fiancée, but that does not mean her reputation is unassailable."

Neville stared at her. "*You* are speaking to *me* about reputation? That's rich. Do not be such a little prude, Cecy. Every matron has her cicisbeo to see to it that she always has an escort to amuse her, to advise her on her appearance, to counsel on the best articles to be found in the best shops in London, and to accompany her to any amusement her heart might desire. In short, to fulfill those functions that husbands are too bored or too busy to take an interest in. If anything, I will enhance her reputation in the way a particularly fine lapdog or an appealing page enhances a lady's social cachet."

Cecilia still looked skeptical.

"The problem with you, Cecy, is that you take everything far too seriously. Not everything is of such momentous importance. Not everything has to have a reason. If every once in a while you did something simply for the sheer enjoyment of it, you would be far better off. All that frowning and fretting is giving you wrinkles, in addition to turning you into a dead bore." Neville flicked an imaginary crumb from his coat, lay down his serviette, and rose to leave.

His sister opened her mouth to retort that if every once in a while her brother did something for a reason, or invested more things in life with momentous importance, they would *all* be better off and she would not have the worries that gave her wrinkles and turned her into a dead bore. But she thought better of it. It was a waste of breath trying to talk sense into Neville—a useless expenditure of energy trying to make him see reason.

"And what is the message you would have me deliver to Miss Wyatt?" Neville glanced in the looking glass over the mantel to assure himself that his cravat was as spotless and as exquisitely arranged as it had been when he left his bed-chamber.

"Just that I am ready for her approval of the results of her final sitting."

"But I am not. I find it quite enchanting to have a charming and beautiful woman haunting my abode on a regular basis." Neville grinned mischievously as, delivering this parting shot, he sailed from the room.

"Neville!" Cecilia half rose from her chair in frustration, but it was too late. Her brother was already gone. And he was just teasing her, anyway.

There was no real harm in Neville, other than his unrelieved commitment to his own amusement and his steadfast refusal to involve himself in anything that brought with it the least hint of responsibility. In years gone by, she had been able to laugh at his antics. What had changed? Had she in fact become the joyless prude he had accused her of being?

Somewhat later in the day, someone whose opinion carried far more weight than her brother's uttered similar sentiments to Cecilia.

"My dear, you really must get out more." Countess Lieven gingerly set down her cup of tea among the clutter of brushes and pots of pigment on the table next to the sofa in Cecilia's studio, as she scanned her friend's face anxiously. "You are working far too hard, and that will only make you dull and cross. If you do not have care, you will end up looking like an antidote. And we would not want that to happen."

"The endless crush of routs and balls would make me dull and cross, not painting. You know that as well as I do."

Dorothea Lieven leaned forward, her narrow, clever face

alight with concern for her friend. "Yes, yes, I know, but balls
and routs are not the only amusements to be had. Just because you find most of the conversations at these affairs
nothing but tedious gossip does not mean that the metropolis
is utterly devoid of intelligent diversions. What about the
opera?"

Cecilia looked skeptical.

"I know, I know. Everyone else attends the opera to see or
be seen, but you could actually listen to the music. That is it!
Come, promise me that you will join us in our box Saturday
evening. It is *La Clemenza di Tito,* which is surely serious
enough even to appeal to your refined tastes. Say you will do
it. I promise you, we shall talk of nothing but the most eru-
dite and stimulating of topics, and we shall be quiet as mice
while the music is being performed."

Cecilia was no proof against such genuine concern so
kindly expressed, but later, after bidding her visitor adieu,
she stared critically at herself in the looking glass. Was she
really a dead bore, as her brother accused her of being—or,
worse yet, at least as far as Dorothea Lieven was concerned,
an antidote?

Yes, there were the faintest lines visible at the corners of
her mouth, and they were not from smiling. Her skin seemed
pale, especially in contrast with the sprinkling of freckles
across her nose, and her eyes looked lifeless. Where was the
clever, energetic girl who had sat dreamy-eyed on the terrace
of the Villa Torloni, listening to the songs of the birds and the
hum of bees as she absorbed the exotic scents, the soft
breezes and the golden Mediterranean sunshine?

When had she stopped enjoying life?

She glanced over to the corner where her picture—so
generously restored to her, and still wrapped in Holland
cloth—was propped up against a pile of canvases. Her lips
tightened as she thought of how it had come to be in the Earl
of Charrington's possession. Everyone else in her life had abdicated their responsibilities, and she had assumed them by

default: that was when she had slowly begun to lose her joie de vivre.

It had not been intentional, of course. She had just begun concentrating on her painting, on turning out portraits to pay the bills, and, eventually, she'd had little time or thought to spare for anything else. And no one—not Neville, not even Dorothea Lieven—seemed to understand that the situation was not of her making. It had not come about because of her choice, but because of necessity.

Nor was anyone really doing anything to help. They could voice all the concerns they wished to voice about her not enjoying herself—her need to find more diversion or amusement in her life—but no one was doing anything to help her find the time or the money to do so. Except one.

A slow smile softened the tense lines of her compressed lips. Sebastian, Earl of Charrington was helping. Preoccupied though he might be—at least according to his fiancée—he understood all the difficulties she was facing, and he was doing his best to help her. Not only by giving her important commissions, but by giving her commissions for work that would challenge her artistic capabilities, spark her interest, and help her grow as an artist and a person. And while it was true that he was giving her more work, instead of offering her the entertainment or diversion that the others were suggesting she so desperately needed, it did not feel like work. She was doing it for herself—for her own growth and satisfaction, to enhance her own reputation—not simply to pay the bills, though the figure he had offered her was certainly handsome enough to pay a cartload of bills.

Thinking of the Earl of Charrington reminded Cecilia that she still had some more measuring to do. What could offer more diversion than a brisk walk to Grosvenor Square on such a lovely day? And what could be better than finding a bit of diversion in the course of fulfilling her obligations?

And perhaps you will see him, a treacherous little voice in her head suggested—a voice that she instantly dismissed as being worse than ridiculous. But it was true that every time she saw the Earl of Charrington, she felt warmed by his friendship and encouraged by his belief in her. In all his conversations with her, he had made it plain that he considered her to be a person worth knowing—a person worth admiring, whose company was both enlightening and enjoyable.

Determined to take at least some pleasure from the walk, Cecilia allowed herself to linger on Bond Street, pausing to look in shop windows here and there and even going so far as to picture herself in a bonnet artfully displayed to its best advantage in the window of Prother and Company. Surely the straw-colored silk lining would be vastly becoming to her, and the green satin trimming and bow would highlight the color of her eyes which, artist that she was, she knew to be her best feature.

Her maid, Susan, accustomed to moving along at a brisk and businesslike pace whenever she accompanied her mistress, glanced at Lady Cecilia curiously. It was certainly not like her to give a second thought to the enticing establishments on Bond Street, much less gaze longingly at bonnets in shop windows almost as though she were considering purchasing such a thing.

The maid was in complete agreement with her mistress, however. The bonnet in question was an enchanting creation with the tips of the feathers dipped in green to match the ribbons, and far too frivolous for a woman who usually insisted on simplicity and, above all, serviceability in her dress. While it was true that Lady Cecilia always presented a picture of quiet elegance, her maid was of the opinion that it verged in the severe, and could be vastly improved with the softening influence of a few seductive feathers or a mildly flirtatious bow now and then.

"There; I *told* Somersworth that higher crowns were all the rage and that no self-respecting husband would allow his wife to appear in a bonnet like the one I am wearing. I look an absolute quiz." A petulant voice interrupted Cecilia's fit of abstraction.

"My dear, you simply cannot expect a gentleman to appreciate these things. Just tell him that you must have it, and there is an end to it. That is what I do with Harleston. He is usually most obliging and happy to indulge me, but he simply has no sense of fashion."

Cecilia had been wondering, somewhat wistfully, what it would be like to purchase a bonnet simply because one wanted it, or because it would make one feel beautiful, without regard for anything else like price or utility. Now, with a queer fluttering of her pulse, she wondered what it would be like to have a gentleman present it to one—a husband, naturally. What would it be like to be handed a box and be told to open it and try it on because *I want to see how lovely you look in it?*

She had never really thought about having a husband before, because she had been so intent on making a way for herself in the world and building her reputation as an artist. Or, if she had thought of it at all, it had been as an encumbrance, something to be avoided because it would take time away from her chosen profession or threaten her hard-won independence. It had simply never occurred to her that having a husband might mean having someone who wanted to indulge her. Being indulged by the right sort of person might actually be quite enjoyable—quite enjoyable, indeed.

Cecilia's breath caught in her throat and her face grew warm at the thought. Then common sense reasserted itself. If one were supremely lucky, one might find such a husband. But why count on luck, which was notoriously fickle, when you could rely on yourself? And that was just what she was doing, and she was proud of herself for doing it.

Holding her head, in its very serviceable bonnet, high, she marched up Bond Street, turned into Brook Street and proceeded at such a pace that by the time she reached Grosvenor Square, she was quite out of breath and so intent on her own thoughts that she nearly collided with the mansion's owner on its steps.

Chapter 18

"Lady Cecilia! How delightful to see you. I was just leaving, but do come in." Sebastian smiled down at her in such a way that all the disturbing thoughts of indulgent gentleman that she had successfully banished during her walk now came rushing back with a vengeance.

"My lord, I did not expect . . . I mean, I only came to take some more measurements. Please do not let me interrupt you."

"On the contrary, I count it extremely fortunate that I did not leave a moment earlier than I did. It is always a pleasure to talk to you. Come, let us go to the ballroom. Mr. Wilkins has just stepped out, but perhaps you will accept my humble assistance as you take your measurements. I do not know exactly, for I am not experienced in such things, but I would venture to guess that measuring goes a great deal more smoothly if two people do it, rather than one."

Cecilia blinked, and then quickly recovered herself. "Why yes, it is easier, and thank you. But surely you have more important things to attend to," she temporized, remembering that the constant unavailability of Barbara's fiancé was Neville's excuse for escorting Barbara to the Egyptian Hall. However, now it certainly did not appear that the Earl of Charrington was too preoccupied with business affairs to pay attention to anything else.

He smiled down at her. "Perhaps some people might think so, but at the moment I cannot think of anything more important to me than assisting you."

Cecilia wondered why she had ever thought him arrogant or cold. She found the charm in his smile truly irresistible, and his interest in everything she did infectious. Furthermore, the look in his eyes as he gave her his arm up the stairs utterly banished all the doubts that had been plaguing her since breakfast. Her brother might consider her an antidote and a dead bore, but the Earl of Charrington made her feel as lovely and as attractive as any Incomparable.

"I am doubly glad to see you today, because it gives me the opportunity to speak to you about the paper by Davy that I gave you. Have you had a chance to read it?"

"I did, but I am sadly afraid that some of it was so technical as to escape me. But I did find the discussion of the reasons for some pigments deteriorating more rapidly than others to be particularly useful. You are disappointed, I see, but I *did* warn you that my talents do not lie in the sciences or mathematics. But tell, me, my lord, what did you think of the paper?"

"I found it most interesting, though to my mind, he did not go far enough."

"Far enough?" Cecilia raised a questioning brow.

"Well, basically, the whole issue of color is even more elemental than the question of pigment, for, elementally speaking, it is a matter of the amount of reflection or refraction of the light on the particles dispersed in the pigment that gives it its color. Therefore, it is not simply a question of the chemical properties of the pigment itself, but of the size of the particles as . . . but I see I am boring you. I often do—bore people, you know. If the truth be told, I am rather a dull fellow."

The sheepish grin that accompanied this admission suddenly made him seem warm, vulnerable, and more endearing than anyone Cecilia had ever met. "No, not at all. It is *I* who am the dull one, I am afraid."

He thought for a moment, and then continued. "Well, to put it simply, the more light that is absorbed, the darker a thing is. Take black, for example; it is not so much a color as the almost total absorption of light, while white reflects almost all of it."

"Yes." She nodded slowly.

"In colored pigments, then, the light is selectively absorbed; it is the reflected light that gives the pigment its hue. So to my mind, color is more a matter of physics than chemistry. It is chemistry that governs such aspects as solubility and stability, which, though they may be of equal importance, are, for me at least, of far less interest."

Cecilia could not help smiling at his earnestness and intensity. His absorption in the question and his eagerness to share it with her were far more charming than all the flattering speeches that he could have made—speeches that most women demanded as a matter of course. Most of the gallants Cecilia had observed over the years were so self-absorbed that the compliments that they paid to the objects of their admiration were not designed to bring pleasure to their recipients so much as to draw attention to the wit and cleverness of the gallant himself.

Such was not the case with the Earl of Charrington. He was genuinely interested in not only the topic, but in her opinion of it, and that interest was far more flattering than any of the Spanish coin she had been offered over the years.

Cecilia tilted her head consideringly for a moment before she responded. "I suppose that, to me, it is more a question of one's feeling about fame and posterity than anything else."

It was Sebastian's turn to look puzzled.

"It seems that much of Sir Humphrey's paper touched on the lasting nature of the pigments used by the ancients. If one is concerned about the immediate effect of one's paint-

ings, then color, or your physics, is most important. If, however, one is thinking not so much of immediate fame, but of
immortality, the durability of the materials one uses is critical, and that is more a matter of chemistry. I myself could
never presume to think that any painting of mine, especially
a portrait, would have value beyond the life of the subject
of the portrait, so I would be forced to admit that physics is
more important to me."

Sebastian regarded her thoughtfully for a moment. "I
have seen the size of the windows in your studio, and the
direction they face. You are obviously accustomed to painting with the best possible light, but you have no way of
knowing how much light will fall on a picture once it has
left your studio. Colors that appear brilliant and jewel-like
in your studio my appear dull and dark when hung over a
mantel in a room with inadequate light. How do you allow
for that?"

Cecilia smiled. There was no doubt that the Earl of Charrington was a very clever and observant gentleman indeed.
"If I am extremely fortunate, I know precisely where the
painting is to be displayed and I can plan accordingly. Otherwise, I must do the best I can by discussing with my patron the location in which the picture is most likely to be
placed, and then hope for the best."

"In that case, would you not prefer to work here where
you will constantly be aware of the play of light and
shadow throughout the day and into the evening? I can certainly arrange to have candles lit in the chandeliers just the
way they would be lit during a ball."

She drew a sharp breath. Here it was again, his offer for
her to have her studio in his house. But she simply could
not spend her days, and perhaps evenings in this room—
the room where he and Barbara would be welcoming and
entertaining their most important guests in the years to
come.

No, it was utterly impossible. She did not wish to think
of it filled with chattering strangers, or, worse yet, with the

Earl holding Barbara in his arms as they waltzed under the thoughtful gaze of *her* paintings, *her* muses. She preferred to have the ballroom remain in her imagination as it was now, large and gracefully proportioned, but empty except for the two of them. "That is very kind of you, but I prefer to work in my own studio, where I am assured of having all my supplies about me."

"Whatever you wish, but if you change your mind, you have only to say the word and I shall have all your supplies brought here. But forgive me, I am taking up too much of your precious time. Let me help you take your measurements."

As they talked, they had moved to stand next to one of the panels to be filled with a painting. Cecilia had pulled the measuring tape out of her reticule before they had become engrossed in conversation. Now as he reached out to take one end of it from her, his fingers accidentally grazed her palm.

It was the lightest of touches, but it was enough to make her tingle all over. The warmth of his touch seemed to flow up her arm to her cheeks and throughout her entire body, galvanizing her and melting her all at the same time.

Barely conscious of what she was doing, Cecilia took the other end of the tape and held it to one pilaster, while he walked to the other and she recorded the figure he gave her.

They proceeded to do the rest of the room in the same way, but she was barely aware of doing so. All of her attention was focused on Sebastian—the way he moved, the fineness of his hands with their long, sensitive fingers, the tilt of his head, the squareness of his jaw, and the look of concentration on his face as he read the figures from the tape. What was it about a simple touch that had made her so intently aware of him, of his sheer physical presence, of the energy that always seemed to radiate from him? And why was she so drawn to him, like a magnet to a lodestone?

At last they were finished and he handed her the tape, which she took gingerly, hastily thrusting it back into her reticule as if she could bury the memory of what a simple touch of his fingers could do to her.

"When we put up the scaffolding, I shall ask Mr. Wilkins to measure the medallion for you. In the meantime, I hope you are satisfied with the results of today."

"What? Oh, yes, the measurements." But she was not satisfied. She was not satisfied at all. She did not want to be mesmerized by this man. She did not want to be so affected by his very touch. She did not want to feel that the two of them shared a special bond that only seemed to grow stronger every time they met. She did not want that at all. She wanted to return to the way it had been before she had met the Earl of Charrington, when nothing and no one disturbed her in this way, where the only two emotions she felt were annoyance with her brother and passion for her art.

No, Cecilia was not satisfied. She wanted his touch to become an embrace, the embrace to become a kiss, the kiss to become . . . but that could never be. What was wrong with her? She had never had thoughts like these before in her life. In fact, she had always denied the very possibility of their existence. How could this be happening to her now?

It was time to leave, to escape the dangerous magic of his presence and return to the safety of her studio, her own little world, where, even if she were not completely satisfied, at least she was in control.

"Thank you. For your assistance, I mean." Even to Cecilia's ears, her words sounded stiff and awkward.

"I was happy to oblige." His eyes still fixed on her, Sebastian moved toward her to take her hand in his. "I enjoyed it very much. I always enjoy our conversations, and I look forward to many more." He raised her hand to his lips, and again the liquid warmth spread throughout her entire body.

Cecilia fought against the dizziness that threatened to overwhelm her, as she tried to extricate her hand with as much dignity as she could muster. "I . . . I must be going."

She turned and fled into the hall, down the stairs, out the

door, and into the street. Susan, who had been waiting for her in the anteroom off the hall, hurried to keep up with her.

She must get home, back to her studio, back to the life she had lived before the Earl of Charrington had come into it, a life which, if it had not been exciting, had at least been calm and well-ordered.

Chapter 19

Entering her studio, Cecilia tore off her bonnet and pelisse and, tossing them onto the sofa, plunged immediately back into her work. With each pencil stroke that filled in the sketch for the first panel in the ballroom, she felt her breathing grow more regular and her pulse slowly return to its normal pace. That was what she needed: work. A few days of sketching and painting would be the perfect antidote to the dangerously upsetting thoughts that kept intruding on her peace of mind.

Work might be the antidote, but only some types of work. She could not, for example, face the nearly completed portrait of Barbara Wyatt, because it only conjured up images of Barbara and Sebastian waltzing together in their gracious ballroom. So the picture, minus the finishing touches, sat on its easel off to one side of the studio.

Involuntarily, Cecilia glanced over in the direction of the shrouded portrait, covered to protect it against the light and possible accidents while she worked on other projects.

In reality, she ought to be grateful to Barbara, for without her steadying presence, Cecilia might find truly herself attracted to the Earl of Charrington—something which she, as a woman who intended to devote the rest of her life to her art, could simply not afford. But with Barbara soon to become his countess, ill-matched though they were, attraction of this sort was simply not an issue.

All her life, Cecilia's only passionate relationship had been with her art. It was the path she had chosen for herself, and nothing had tempted her to stray from it, until now. It had allowed her to remain coolly unaffected by anyone and everyone, blissfully secure in the belief that it would always be that way. Now, much to her horror, she had discovered that it was not necessarily so. But fortunately, the person who had so recently entered her life and turned it upside down would soon be leaving it.

Cecilia bit her lip and went back to her drawing, taking herself severely to task for inadvertently allowing herself to be distracted by thoughts of the Earl of Charrington.

But she was soon interrupted by a distraction of another and less pleasant sort. Just as the clock was striking two, Neville sauntered into the studio, a picture of sartorial splendor in biscuit-colored pantaloons, an exquisitely cut coat of Bath superfine, gleaming Hessians, and a snowy cravat artfully arranged *en cascade*.

"You can put up your brushes and paints now, Cecy—your days of scrimping and saving are gone forever." He spoke in his usual breezy manner, but there was a hint of self-consciousness in his tone that made his sister scrutinize him warily.

"And why is that? I have no intention of giving up my *brushes and paints*, as you call them. But I would not mind not having to worry about bills."

"There, see?" Neville beamed. "You are always complaining that you are the responsible one. Now someone else is going to take over that responsibility."

"You cannot tell me that you—"

"You and all your bills will be your husband's responsibility now."

A cold wave of fear swept over Cecilia. "My husband? What husband? Neville, you *know* I have no wish to be married."

"I know, I know, but this is different. Melmouth bears one of the most ancient and honorable titles in the country. He is rich beyond our wildest dreams, and he is not some young man who still has his wild oats to sow."

"No, he is an old reprobate who is still sowing his wild oats. Neville, are you all about in the head? I would *never* marry such a person as Lord Melmouth. I would never marry anyone," she added hastily.

"But you *have* to marry him, Cecy."

"No, Neville, I do not *have* to do anything."

"I shall be ruined otherwise."

His sister's eyes narrowed suspiciously. "And why would that be?"

"I lost everything to him last night at White's. Well, not everything, but ten thousand pounds might as well be everything. I've done all that I can to raise the wind, but the estate is already mortgaged to the hilt, and the rent we are getting from the tenants is already spent. The damn cent-percenters will not even talk to me, much less lend me money at a ruinous rate."

"Ten thousand pounds?" Cecilia paled. It would take her years to earn that much money. And even then, she might not succeed in doing so. "And why not ignore this debt as you ignore every other one?" she asked bitterly.

"Because tradesmen's bills are one thing, but debts of honor are quite another. You cannot be serious, Cecy!"

"Apparently not. But I fail to see what all this has to do with my marrying Melmouth."

"Because he agreed to forgive the debt if I would consent to your marrying him."

"I hesitate to point out, Neville, that your consent has absolutely nothing to do with it. Mine, however, has everything to do with it, and I shall not consent to marry anyone at all, much less an aging roué. How could you, Neville?"

"But Cecy"—his voice was pleading now—"I shall be ruined otherwise. All you have to do is give Melmouth an heir, and then you are free to paint to your heart's content—

or whatever else you want to do—in the most elegant of circumstances, without having to bother yourself about money again."

"There is no such thing as never having to bother about money again. Fortunes, as you very well know, can be won or lost on the turn of a card or the roll of the dice, and even respectable inheritances like ours once was can disappear at a very rapid rate. No, I simply shall not do it."

"But Cecy, I am a ruined man!"

Her face softened. Neville was irresponsible, irritating, and more than a little shallow, but he was still her brother. "I said I would not marry him. I did not say I would not repay your debt."

"But Cecy, how can you? Papa sold Mama's jewelry long ago, and the rent on Shelburne Hall is not due until next quarter day, and all that goes for this anyway." He waved his hand disparagingly at the studio.

"Never mind, I shall think of something. But marriage is absolutely out of the question. Now go away and let me think."

But all the thinking in the world was not going to remedy the situation. She had no money, only the power to earn it. But earn it she would, even if it took years to pay back her brother's debt. There was nothing for it but to speak to Lord Melmouth herself—to plead with him, if necessary, to allow her to pay back the money a little at a time.

There was no time like the present to speak to him, and Cecilia was a firm believer in dealing with the unpleasantnesses in life immediately. But, impatient as she was to get the interview over, she knew she could not hope to find his lordship at home at that hour, so she was forced to summon up all the patience she could muster, and wait until the next morning to call on him, regardless of how it might look. Of course she would take Susan with her, but still it was not the thing for a woman to call on a man like Lord Melmouth—not even a woman of a certain age who was a professional painter.

Lord Melmouth was a close enough acquaintance of her brother's that Sedley, who had delivered the occasional message from her brother to him, was able to give her his direction in Upper Brook Street. "I shall be happy to deliver a message for you, too, if you wish, my lady," the footman volunteered when she asked him for it.

"Thank you, Sedley," Cecilia's mouth set in a grim line of determination, "but this is one message I prefer to deliver myself."

That determination faltered the next day, however, when she found herself on the steps of Lord Melmouth's discreetly elegant town house. Discreetly elegant though his house might be, there was nothing discreetly elegant about his reputation, and Cecilia could not ignore the misgivings that rose inside her as she reluctantly climbed the steps.

Cecilia had only seen the man once at the theater, when Neville—in an expansive mood after a successful night at faro—had treated her to a box. Lord Melmouth had called on them in their box and insisted on an introduction to Cecilia, though it should have been clear to even the most obtuse of observers that she had eyes only for the action on stage and not for the dissipated older gentleman who eyed her with such patent approval.

She had taken an instant disliking to him then and there. The stories she had subsequently heard about his whoring and his mistresses, his obsession with gambling of any sort—cards, the turf, the fancy—had done nothing to improve her impression of him. In fact, the only thing that could be said in Melmouth's favor was that, gamble though he did constantly, he only succeeded in winning and adding to the vast fortune he had inherited from a legendarily parsimonious father.

No, Lord Melmouth was not the sort of man on whom Lady Cecilia Manners was likely to waste the time of day, much less consider bestowing her hand in marriage. And as Susan lifted the heavy brass knocker on the forbidding-looking door, Cecilia did her best to suppress an involuntary shudder at the thought of even being in the same room with the man. But now was not the time to be missish—not when her brother's very existence, not to mention her own, was at stake.

Chapter 20

The knocker had barely thudded against its plate when the door was opened by a tall, cadaverous-looking man who did not blink an eye at the spectacle of two young women on his master's doorstep.

"Do not let me out of your sight, Susan," Cecilia whispered as the man disappeared to inform his lordship that he had a visitor.

Following orders to the letter, Susan took a seat in the hall outside the library, to which the butler conducted her mistress.

"Lady Cecilia, what a delightful surprise—and one that I hope will often be repeated, now that our acquaintance is to be on much more, ah, *intimate* terms." Lord Melmouth rose from his desk and came forward to bow low over Cecilia's hand as she entered the room. His bottle-green coat was exquisitely cut, but the buttons were just a trifle too large for true elegance, and the yellow pantaloons a shade too colorful.

These were the most fleeting of impressions, however, for it was his face that gave Cecilia the deepest pause. Pale blue eyes, bloodshot from late nights at the gaming table, and a complexion lined with dissipation and of an unhealthy tint that betrayed a lifetime of self-indulgence, did nothing to alleviate her dismay.

His smile—self-satisfied and with a hint of the predator about it—only made matters worse. "And how, pray tell, may I be of service to you? Not that I do not welcome visits from lovely young ladies at any time, but, never having been visited by you before—even though you are to be my wife—I would venture to guess that this is not a social call."

Cecilia refused the chair he offered her with a graceful flourish, but stood gripping the back instead as she fought to gain control over the nausea that threatened to overwhelm her. "My lord, I very much fear that you are laboring under something of a misapprehension."

Lord Melmouth grinned slyly. "I rather doubt it, my dear, for I am a man whose vast experience in, ah, *worldly* affairs has left me little inclined to have faith or trust in anything; therefore I never count on a thing unless it is an absolute certainty."

A cold shiver slithered down Cecilia's spine, but with a supreme effort she managed to remain icily calm. "I understand that my brother owes you a large sum of money."

Lord Melmouth stroked his chin, eyeing her appreciatively. Not many who found themselves in his power were able to remain as coolly detached as the self-possessed young lady before him. His first impression of Lady Cecilia Manners had been entirely correct: she was indeed a woman of proud and independent spirit. He liked women of spirit— all the more challenging to tame, and all the more thrilling the victory when they finally fell victim to him. Not only was she a woman of spirit, but she was clearly a good deal more clever than her self-indulgent fool of a brother.

"Not *just* a large sum of money," he replied silkily, "but a debt of honor. There is a vast difference between the two, as you no doubt realize."

"I have come to repay that debt."

"Have you now, indeed?" His tone was one of polite interest, but there was no mistaking the cold refusal in his eyes.

Cecilia reached into her reticule, but his voice, cold and mocking, stopped her. "Do not bother, my dear. I doubt that you have enough money even to catch my interest. The entire sum that your brother owes me is truly paltry to me. What does interest me, however, is you. Or to be more precise, what you can give me: an heir whose parentage is beyond reproach."

Try as she would, Cecilia could not control the look of disgust that flitted across her face.

He laughed when he saw it. "It is difficult to believe, is it not, that, jaded as I am, I find myself longing at this stage in life for someone who will carry on my name—someone to whom I can leave all the worldly goods I have acquired over the years, someone—"

"Never! You may threaten my brother, our family, with dishonor—ruin, if you wish to call it—but you cannot make me do anything I do not wish to do, and you certainly cannot make me marry you!" Cecilia spun on her heel and, without a backward glance, strode from the room her shoulders back and her head held high.

She marched down the stairs and out into the street, trusting that the faithful Susan was following close behind her.

In fact, she did not even pause to draw breath until she had reached North Audley Street. Only then did the red mist of anger that was swirling before her eyes clear enough for her to realize where she was; in a public place, striding along like a mad thing, raising curious glances from passersby.

"Oh my lady." Gasping for breath, Susan at last caught up with her mistress. "Are you all right? That dreadful man has upset you, but he cannot harm you, can he?" The maid looked anxiously at her mistress, her round, honest face the very picture of distress and concern.

"No, Susan," Cecilia muttered grimly. "He is not going to harm me. He is not even going to upset me if I can help it.

Now you go on home. I must clear my head. I must think, and I cannot do it with you hovering over me. I know you only have my best interests at heart, and I bless you for that, but I need to be alone."

"But, my lady, you should not be alone. And besides, whatever will people think?"

"I am sure that if my brother and Lord Melmouth were bandying my name about at White's, my reputation will become so unsavory that it will matter very little what people think. With any luck, it will become so unsavory that marriage to me will be out of the question for a man who longs for a wife of irreproachable lineage who can give him the respectable heir he covets."

"But, my lady . . ." Susan caught sight of the determined glint in her mistress' eye, and the protest died in her throat. "Very well, my lady." And with only a few worried glances, Susan scuttled off, leaving her mistress to continue on at a more leisurely pace.

With Susan gone, and now that her initial spurt of anger had worn off, Cecilia was suddenly overcome with the effrontery, the sheer disgust of it all. That such a man had even thought of her, a woman he barely knew, in such terms—especially when she had never considered him anything but repulsive—was almost more than she could bear.

Hot tears scalded her eyelids, and for a moment she could not see a thing in front of her. Blinking rapidly, she gulped and tried to clear her field of vision before she continued on her way, but it was already too late, for there in front of her, too close to ignore, was the Earl of Charrington.

"Lady Cecilia!" Anxious eyes swept her face. "My poor girl, whatever is the matter?"

"I . . . I . . ."

"Here, come inside." Sebastian had just been descending the steps of his house when he had caught sight of her. He realized instantly that something unpleasant had happened, for Lady Cecilia Manners was not the sort of person to become upset over a trifling incident.

Grasping her elbow with a steadying hand, he led her inside into the small anteroom off the entrance hall. "Now then, what has occurred to upset you?"

There was nothing for it but to tell him. With his hand warm and comforting under her elbow, his eyes dark with concern for her, Cecilia found herself telling him everything that had just occurred.

He remained silent as she spoke, all his attention fixed on her, but she found his very silence reassuring, and the recounting of her tale strangely calming. He knew her, knew what sort of person she was. He knew what a horrible insult Melmouth's offer was to her sense of independence and self-reliance. She explained the situation coolly, rationally, not leaving out any of the facts, unpleasant as they were, and no matter how poorly they reflected on her brother.

It was not until she reached the end when she repeated Melmouth's words, *What does interest me, however, is you. Or to be more precise, what you can give me: an heir*, that she faltered. A wave of indignation and disgust rose up in her. Her lips quivered in spite of her determination to remain calm, and her eyes filled with hot, angry tears. "He . . . he would not even look at my money. In fact, I do not think he ever intended to collect the money from me or Neville. The . . . the . . ." Words failed her.

"My poor girl," Sebastian whispered as he drew her into his arms, "my poor darling."

It was too much. Cecilia broke down and sobbed unrestrainedly into his shoulder while he held her in a comforting embrace.

At last her sobs subsided and she was able to catch her breath. Sniffing prosaically, she fished inside her reticule, pulled out a handkerchief, and dabbed angrily at her tear-soaked lashes. "I beg your pardon. Ordinarily I am not such a watering pot, but when I think of how I struggled all those years to support myself independently so I could remain free to devote myself to my painting, I cannot help being furious

at having it all taken away just because, just because . . ."
Once again, her voice was suspended by tears.

"Cecilia, listen to me." Sebastian had released her the instant she began hunting for her handkerchief, but now he pulled her back into his arms. "It will not happen. I swear to you that nothing will happen. Believe me."

He sounded so sure of himself. He looked so solid and reassuring that she wanted to believe him. But she had believed in other men before—her father, even Neville to some degree—and she had been bitterly disappointed every time. "But how?"

He cupped her chin in his hand, forcing her to look up at him, to see the sincerity in his eyes, to hear the conviction in his voice. "Believe me. I promise you. Nothing will happen."

He bent his head and pressed his lips to hers.

The kiss was only meant to prove to her the truth of his words, to seal his promise to her that he would not let any harm come to her or her brother, but suddenly it blossomed into something much more.

As his lips touched hers, all his pent-up feelings for this incredible woman came rushing to the surface—appreciation for her courage, admiration of her talent and her independence, sympathy for her drive to learn and grow and succeed, concern for her happiness . . . along with feelings he never knew he possessed—tenderness and an indefinable longing to share everything with her, the woman who had always seemed to be his kindred spirit.

Her mouth was warm and inviting, and he could feel her breath upon his lips, her heart beating against his. He pulled her closer to him, and gave himself up to the longing, forgetting everything else in the world except the heady feeling of holding her in his arms at last.

His hands slid down the curve of her neck, and caressed the delicate softness of her skin. He breathed in the scent of rosewater, and realized that he had been waiting for this moment—longing for this since the day her picture had called out to him from the print shop window in the Strand. From then on she had belonged to him. Since that moment, they had been soul mates.

But he belonged to someone else. Sebastian groaned inwardly and gently, slowly, agonizingly withdrew his lips from hers and set her away from him. "Please, I did not mean . . . I only meant . . . I simply want you to know that I care what happens to you, and that I will not let harm befall you." It sounded impossibly stilted and awkward, but he meant very word of it, with all his heart.

Cecilia smiled tremulously and nodded. "I know." She raised one gloved hand to touch her lips, as if she had suddenly discovered their existence. She touched his cheek ever so gently. "Thank you. I . . . I had better go. Susan will wonder what has become of me." And then, as if she had never been there, as if the magic between them had never happened, she vanished back out into the street.

Chapter 21

This time, however, instead of striding furiously along, Cecilia seemed to float slowly along a few inches above the ground, unaware that her feet were moving beneath her.

All she could think of, all she could feel was the touch of his lips burning on hers, the warmth of his hands at her waist, the soft caress of his fingers on her cheek, and the reassurance of his arms around her.

But it was more than comfort and reassurance that his kiss had given her. It had evoked a yearning in her that Cecilia had never felt before, a desperate longing to be one with him, to be part of him, to feel as close to him physically as she felt mentally and emotionally—a yearning that could never be satisfied, because he was soon to be married to another woman.

The pain of this simultaneous discovery and loss hit her like a physical blow, bringing Cecilia to a standstill in the middle of Bond Street. Fashionable shoppers swirled around her as she struggled to catch her breath, her heart pounding in her chest. She had never felt so alive or so at a loss.

All her life, Cecilia had been sure of where she was going and what she wanted. Practically from the moment she had been able to grasp a piece of chalk or a pencil she had wanted to draw, and then to paint. Her father had always encouraged her in this desire, bringing in drawing masters and then artists from the Neapolitan court to teach her and advise her. He took her from palaces to churches to Roman ruins so she could observe and learn from the best examples of artistic endeavor that the world had to offer.

With her pencils and sketchbook or her palette and brushes as her companions, she had never been lonely, never felt at a loss for company or diversion, even though she had never had any schoolmates or friends of her age with which to share her hopes and dreams, her childish secrets. And she had not felt the lack of any of it, for she always had her art. Until now, that is, when suddenly having discovered life's incredible possibilities—possibilities of which she had been completely ignorant—she felt bereft and at a loss as to how to proceed.

Take hold of yourself, my girl, she admonished herself severely. *Thousands upon thousands of women are kissed every day without falling into a decline. It was a simple gesture of comfort and nothing more.*

But in her heart of hearts, she knew it was more than that—much, much more. It was the distillation of all that she had felt about Sebastian, Earl of Charrington, from the moment she had bumped into him in the vestibule of Somerset House and discovered the passionate man beneath the self-assured financier. They were two of a kind. They were soul mates.

And now, having proven that to herself, she must do her very best to forget it, or it would destroy her.

There was only one thing she could do: fling herself back into her art, bury herself so deeply in her painting that the rest of the world would cease to exist.

So determined was she to do this that when Cecilia reached Golden Square, she did not even bother to remove her bonnet or her pelisse, but went straight to her sketchbook and opened it to the still-evolving drawing of Cupid and Psyche.

She stared fixedly at it for a few moments. It was an improvement over the first attempt, but it was still too stiff. There was not enough feeling in the picture, and no electricity between the two of them. Now she knew what it felt like to burn at another's touch, to long to be joined to that other person for all time, to mingle his breath with her own, to feel his heart beat next to hers until it was a single beat between the two of them. That was it! That was what the picture was still missing, despite her work on it. Cecilia began sketching furiously.

She was so wrapped up in her sketching that she had no idea how long she had been drawing when she heard laughter and voices in the hallway, and it wasn't until she tried to move her cramped limbs and pry open her fingers that she realized it must have been a very long time indeed.

There was another burst of laughter, and then the door to the studio flew open, revealing Neville and Barbara—a Barbara who looked even more radiant than usual in a most becoming bonnet with a straw-colored silk lining, green ribbons, and feathers dipped in green to match the ribbons.

Cecilia drew a harsh, painful breath. Had Barbara's fiancé also seen the bonnet in the window on Bond Street, and purchased it for her knowing how ravishing she would look in it?

As a woman whose talent had provided her with the opportunity to make her own way in the world, Cecilia almost never envied other less talented women. Now, however, she suffered a rare pang of jealousy. Surely Barbara Wyatt, who had only to ask for a luxury to have it bestowed upon her, had no need of yet another bonnet, especially that particular one—a bonnet that would have been so very becoming on someone else who had also admired it in the shop window.

Cecilia barely had time to reproach herself for this unworthy thought when Barbara, who never noticed anything about anyone but herself, patted the bonnet with a self-satisfied smile. "I see that you are admiring my bonnet. Is it not the sweetest thing? I saw it in a window on Bond Street yesterday, and I just had to have it. Of course it was shockingly dear, and I am sure Papa will put me on bread and water for a week for being so extravagant when I have already spent my entire allowance for this quarter, but there was simply no living without it."

"In fact, it would have been a crime indeed for such a bonnet not to grace a head as beautiful as yours." Neville added gallantly.

Cecilia slowly let out the breath she was not even aware she had been holding. So Sebastian had *not* bought it for her! Suddenly she felt quite lighthearted, even joyous with the relief of it all.

"As always, you are too kind, my lord." Completely ignoring Cecilia, Barbara directed a playful smile at Neville.

"Never. Why, I am the soul of honesty where you are concerned."

"Then does that mean you make it a regular practice to lie to others?" she asked, a coquettish gleam in her eye.

"Would you have me be unkindly truthful instead? I am a peaceful fellow, you know, and I have an absolute horror for bluntness. There are so few true beauties in the world that one must either rely on half-truths and equivocation, or be cruelly honest. I prefer to live in harmony with my fellow creatures, which is why I prefer to spend my time in the company of someone like you, for example, whose beauty I can admire with all honesty and candor. I consider myself doubly fortunate today for having encountered such a vision of loveliness on my doorstep. Usually one has to search the world over to find such a treasure."

"And what, may I ask, has brought this vision to our doorstep?" Even to her own ears, Cecilia's voice sounded in acid contrast to her brother's smooth-tongued phrases, but the flirtatious exchange between the two of them was making her extremely uncomfortable—more for Sebastian's sake than her own. Unsophisticated though she might be, Cecilia somehow did not feel that it was right for a young woman so soon to be married to an exceedingly handsome and eligible man to be talking, laughing, and looking at an-

other man in a manner that could only be described as intimate.

"What?" Interrupted in the middle of this mutually satis-
factory exchange, the pair of them stared blankly at Cecilia.

Barbara was the first to recover. "Before I was so distracted by this too-charming gentleman here, you mean?"
She darted a saucy glance at Neville. "I was on my way to
inquire about my portrait, which must be nearly finished by
now."

"Finished? What a question!" Neville raised his eyebrows in exaggerated surprise. "A portrait of Miss Wyatt
will never be finished. No artist, no matter how talented, can
capture the loveliness, the liveliness—"

"No, sirrah, you must stop," Barbara interrupted, laughing. "In spite of your claims to rigorous honesty where I am
concerned, you are now clearly offering me Spanish coin."

"Indeed, I am not." Neville looked hurt. "How can you
doubt me, when you only have to look in this glass." Taking
her elbow he steered her toward the looking glass over the
mantel. "See how honest I am being?" He smiled at both
their reflections. "Can you honestly look in this glass and
tell me you have seen anything lovelier in quite some time?"

Then, still holding her arm, he led her to the portrait by
the window and, whipping off the covering, he waved dramatically at the picture before her. "Even this, splendidly
executed though it may be, is but a pale reflection of reality.
Sadly, though, it is all I have to console me when I am not
looking at the real thing. And soon I shall even be deprived
of that small consolation for as you see, it is almost finished." He paused and smiled deep into Barbara's eyes.

"Ahem." Cecilia joined the couple at the easel. "As my
brother says, it is nearly finished—there is just the varnish-
ing left to be done, unless your fiancé has any corrections or
additions. I hope he will be pleased with the result."

"Who? Oh, Charrington. Yes, I am sure he will be satisfied." Barbara dismissed her fiancé with a wave of her hand.
"As long as it is an accurate representation, I am sure he will

be satisfied. Accuracy and facts and figures, that is all that matters to him. So very dull."

Cecilia refrained from pointing out to Barbara that it was her fiancé's appreciation of art, and especially of portraiture, that was responsible for her presence in the studio in the first place. If the Earl of Charrington's fiancée did not have the temperament to appreciate his taste and aesthetic sensibilities, then it was not Cecilia's role to point it out to her. Besides, the way the beauty was smiling at Neville, Cecilia very much doubted that anything she might say would make any impression at all on either one of them.

She was desperately casting about for some way to bring the two of them to their senses when there was a rap on the door, and Sedley appeared bearing a tray of biscuits and glasses of ratafia. "Begging your pardon, my lady, but his lordship asked that I bring refreshments to the studio."

"And rightly so. Thank you, Sedley. Do sit down, Miss Wyatt, and tell me what you think of the picture." Recovering her wits at last, Cecilia waved to a chair by the fireplace and took the other, leaving Neville to fend for himself as best he could on the sofa. "As I say, I am almost ready to apply the varnish, so if there is anything you wish changed, you must tell me now."

Barbara glanced hastily at the portrait. "No, it all seems in order to me."

In the face of Cecilia's coolly professional tone, she had far less to say than when encouraged by her brother's admiring glances. "I only stopped in for the briefest of moments, for I am due at home for a fitting. Madame Céleste is so much in demand that it would never do to be late. One is an absolute slave to these creatures, but if one is to keep up one's reputation for elegance, there is simply nothing to be done about it. I am sure that your brother is in perfect agreement with me."

She shot a conspiratorial glance at Neville as she set down her glass and rose to leave. "I do hope we will see you at the opera tomorrow evening. Charrington will simply have to agree to attend, for I am told that everyone who is anyone is likely to be there."

Flashing another enchanting smile that was clearly all for Neville's benefit, she was gone before either of them could see her to the door.

Chapter 22

Cecilia's eyes narrowed suspiciously as she turned to look at her brother. "The opera tomorrow evening? I gather from the speaking look Miss Wyatt directed at you that you mentioned the Lieven's invitation to us to share their box."

"But of course, dear sister. Just because you wish to hide yourself away in your hole of a studio is no reason for me to isolate myself from the rest of society, and if I wish to see as many acquaintances as possible when I attend the opera, why then, I shall. And such a delightful acquaintance as it is too." Neville raised a provocative eyebrow.

"My studio is *not* a hole, and this flirtation with Miss Wyatt must be stopped."

"But, Cecy, the poor girl is quite plainly perishing from boredom and neglect, thanks to that dullard of a fiancé of hers."

"He is not a dullard, which she would discover if she were to interest herself in anything at all besides the latest fashion. At any rate, however, her amusement should not be furnished by you. It is not proper."

"Why, sister, what a little prude you have become. Or is it only your own acquaintance with the Earl of Charrington that makes you rush to his defense in such a vehemently moralistic fashion? It is not the least attractive, you know. But then, town tabbies never are."

"I am *not* a town tabby, and I do not set myself up as an arbiter of other people's morals. You *know* I do not, Neville. But in this case, when it involves the happiness and welfare of a hardworking and honorable gentleman, then yes, I am concerned."

"An *honorable gentleman*," Neville mused. "Well that is certainly an interesting way of putting it."

"The Earl of Charrington most certainly *is* an honorable gentleman. He has done his best to honor both his friendship and his debt of gratitude to Sir Richard Wyatt by marrying his only daughter, and he has honored my talent by giving me not only the chance to paint his fiancée's portrait, but by offering me the opportunity to try my hand at more ambitious paintings in his ballroom, which will not only increase my reputation, but our fortunes as well."

"Which we would not be needing if this *honorable gentleman* were not responsible for our ruin in the first place."

"Ruin? What ever do you mean? Before he came to commission the portrait of Miss Wyatt, I barely knew his name, much less ever set eyes on him."

"You may not have, but Papa did—and to his utter destruction, I might add."

"*What?* That is absurd! Papa lost all his money playing cards because he was bored and miserably unhappy having to live in a society that lacked culture, taste, an appreciation for art, and all those other things he was forced to leave behind when we left Naples."

"And who, dear sister, do you suppose was responsible for relieving him of that boredom and our fortune as well? Who, but his constant playing companion, a man who knew that Papa was easily enough beaten by a clever opponent? Who but the exceedingly clever, mathematically inclined, but naturally *honorable* Earl of Charrington?"

"I do not believe it!" Cecilia's hand crept to her throat in horror as she recalled her brother's saying some time ago that the Earl of Charrington possessed a truly formidable reputation at cards. It was only natural that her father, who sought the best in every field would have been drawn to such a skilled gambler. But surely Sebastian had known her father was not a worthy opponent. And knowing that, surely he would have refused to take advantage of it? An *honorable gentleman* certainly would have refused to play with him.

"How can you be so sure? Papa spent his entire life in the gaming rooms at Brooks's and White's. He must have played against hundreds of opponents."

"I can be sure because I saw the stacks of vowels made out to Charrington on his dressing table one day, and he admitted to me that he simply could not win against a man who was such a genius at cards. Since then I have heeded his advice and stayed away from Charrington."

"And so you played against Melmouth instead! Oh, I don't know why I even listen to you . . . or anyone. I am sick to death of the lot of you." Stifling a sob, Cecilia slammed out of the studio, leaving her brother to stare after her, a curiously arrested expression in his bright blue eyes.

"So that is the way the wind blows, is it?" He muttered quietly under his breath. Then whistling, softly he sauntered off to the more congenial atmosphere of Watier's where he did not run the risk of encountering either Melmouth, who patronized White's, or Charrington, who was only to be found at Brooks's.

In fact, he might have spared himself the trouble, for at that particular moment, neither gentleman was at either club. They were both enduring a singularly unpleasant moment in Lord Melmouth's richly appointed library in Upper Brook Street.

At least, Lord Melmouth was enduring an uncomfortable moment under the implacable gaze of the Earl of Charrington, who himself was merely disgusted at having to breathe the same air as the despicable old roué.

"There is no discussion to be had, Melmouth. You will

tear up that vowel, eliminating the Marquess of Shelburne's debt and freeing Lady Cecilia from your barbarous intentions."

"Come, come, now, Charrington, we are men of the world. We both know that when Lady Cecilia becomes the Countess of Melmouth, she will have an infinitely better life than she does now. As mistress of vast estates, she will have servants and carriages, and generous pin money at her instant command, whereas now she has a very limited existence eking out her living in inferior quarters in Golden Square. Why, not only will she be saving her brother's precious reputation, she will be winning for herself a most advantageous position in the bargain. She has everything to gain and nothing to lose."

"Except her freedom, her pride, and her independence, not to mention the distinct disadvantage of being forced to endure living under the same roof with a scoundrel."

Lord Melmouth leapt to his feet, his face suffused with rage. "You will take that back, Charrington! What right do you have to come storming in here like some *preux chevalier* defending a lady's honor? I have offered her the protection of my name. You have no right to look down your disdainful nose at me. *I* have not sullied my family's name by going into trade."

"No, you have not." The earl's voice was steely. "Indeed, you sell your canal shares and mining shares so immediately after you win them from your poor benighted victims, and at such an enormous profit, that one wonders if you plan it all well in advance."

"I . . . I . . ." The color drained from Lord Melmouth's face as he gasped for breath.

"Precisely." Sebastian smiled with grim satisfaction. "Now, Melmouth, if you do not want it voiced around the clubs of St. James's, or in the City for that matter, that you are plucking innocent pigeons in the hope of gaining their shares at a most advantageous discount, then I suggest you hand over the Marquess of Shelburne's vowel immediately and give up all notion of finding yourself a countess anytime soon."

"You are nothing but a common blackmailer, Charrington. You won't get away with this. I shall see to it that you are no longer welcome at any club in London. It should be easy enough, once I call into question the reputation of a man who wins at cards as easily as you do," Melmouth snarled.

But he went to his desk and withdrew a crumpled note covered with the Marquess of Shelburne's nearly illegible scrawl. "There. Take it and be damned, you meddling fool. You'll get no thanks from Shelburne for saving his good name and leaving him with that bluestocking of a sister on his hands."

Stuck in an untenable situation, the Earl of Melmouth was forced to look for satisfaction wherever he could find it, and he was able to derive at least a little bit from the murderous expression that his last sally had sparked in his unwelcome visitor's eyes. "You have what you came for, Charrington, now get out of here before I call my man and have him throw you out."

It was the last taunt of a man who had been utterly defeated, and they both new it.

Sebastian took the vowel, turned on his heel, and left without deigning to reply.

The interview had been no more unpleasant than he had anticipated, and it had, in fact, been settled more quickly than he had dared hope. He wished that he could go straight away to break the news to Cecilia, but he did not wish to run the risk of telling her when Neville was there. For as much as he wanted to free the sister from an impossible situation, he did not want to cause the brother shame or embarrassment by doing so.

Not that Neville did not deserve to be embarrassed. That was the very least of the punishment he deserved for his selfish pursuit of pleasure and indulgence at the expense of his sister's peace of mind, not to mention her hard-won independence.

No, Sebastian was afraid that if he were to encounter the Marquess of Shelburne at this particular moment, he might be tempted to give him such a piece of his mind that not even his sister would welcome Sebastian into their household any time soon. And that was something that he simply could not risk.

Sebastian had come to look forward to—no, to depend upon—seeing Cecilia on a regular basis. Even when she had been nothing more to him than a picture on his wall, she had brightened his days. Now she filled his thoughts and his heart to a dangerous degree. Every interesting thing he learned, every problem he encountered, every solution he proposed, he wondered what she would think of it. Would she agree with him or disagree, and what new perspective would her artist's eye, her clever brain, or her knowledge of other places and other cultures reveal that he had not seen? Would she then smile at his blindness and share her thoughts with him in a way that made him feel appreciated and enjoyed as he had never been appreciated or enjoyed before in his life?

Chapter 23

The Marquess of Shelburne's canceled vowel arrived at Golden Square inside a note addressed to Lady Cecilia Manners just as Sedley was about to bring in the morning post to his master and mistress at the breakfast table. Sedley took the note from Sebastian's footman and added it to the pile of correspondence.

It lay on top of the letters from friends in Europe and tradesmen's bills demanding Cecilia's attention, the bold, forceful script compelling her to open it up and read the words inside: *You are free.*

Cecilia gave an involuntary gasp and dropped the note as if it were a hot poker. The vowel fluttered to the floor.

His sister's gasp made Neville look up from his buttered eggs to see the blood draining from her face. Curious, he picked up the piece of paper that had floated under the breakfast table. "I say, that is a bit of luck, isn't it? I wonder—"

"I do not wonder at all," his sister hissed, rising so rapidly that her chair nearly fell over. "And it won't do! I tell you, I will not have it. I will pay back every penny myself if it takes the rest of my life to do so."

"Will not have what, Cecy? What ever are you doing?"

But Cecilia was gone before Neville could finish his sen-

tence, only to sweep past the breakfast room not two minutes later wearing her bonnet and pelisse.

"And where ever are you going?" Neville called after
her, as he sat gazing at her retreating figure in utter bewil-
derment. Carefully folding the vowel, he stuck it in his
pocket. It was a great deal too bad that he had been unsuc-
cessful in marrying his sister off to a fortune, but his debt
was canceled, so he would not repine. In fact, he might
even reward himself by seeing what was on the auction
block today at Tattersall's. He had not been able to touch
anything from Crompton's stable when he had sold up, and
it really was a long time since he had had a new hack.

Meanwhile, his sister was in a far less celebratory mood.
She had spent an utterly sleepless night fighting a sense of
betrayal and loss as great, if not greater, than she had when
her father had died. The Marquess of Shelburne's slow decline and mounting gambling losses had at least forewarned
her of the disaster that was about to befall them. But there
had been no warning this time, and the resulting pain that
came from the discovery of Sebastian's perfidy was as sear-
ing and unexpected as if someone had suddenly stabbed her
in the heart.

Which is precisely what had happened that morning,
metaphorically speaking, she concluded as, sighing
wearily, she watched dawn creep slowly across the sky after
a night of restless misery.

Sebastian, the one person she had come to trust as much
as she trusted herself, had proven himself unworthy of that
trust. Like her, he had appeared to have no patience with the
falsity and pretense that so much of the fashionable world
seemed to accept as a matter of course. Like her, he appeared to place value in hard work and tasks accomplished
rather than outward appearance and social reputation. Like
her, he had endured a ruined father and struggled to regain
hopelessly mortgaged estates. How could he, then, have
failed to admit to her that he had known her father—known
him to the extent that he had become an instrument in his

downfall? How could he care for her and yet keep the truth hidden from her all at the same time?

At least she had thought he had cared, thought she had read it in the warmth and concern in his dark eyes, seen it in the special half-smile he reserved only for her, sensed it in the intensity of his interest in her hopes and dreams, his very real support for her work, and felt it in that brief but unforgettable kiss. But perhaps she had been wrong, deluding herself into believing that he cared for her simply because she cared so much for him, cared for the pain and loneliness he had suffered as a boy, admired the resourcefulness and courage that had driven him to rebuild his fortune and live a productive life so different from that of his father and the rest of his peers. She cared for him as a kindred spirit, as someone who understood her view of the world as no one else had ever understood it before.

What a fool she had been, deluded by the magic of his touch, and a kiss that had transported her into a world of feelings and desire she had never known existed. Well, she had awakened from that delusion now. All that was left was to tell him that she had.

But when the butler ushered her into the library of the slim house in Curzon Street, and Sebastian rose from his desk to greet her—that special smile of welcome on his face and an oddly intense light in his eyes—her resolution failed her. The sight of the broad shoulder that she had cried on and the strong arms that had held and comforted her made her dizzy with the same nameless longing that had overwhelmed her when they had kissed.

"Lady Cecilia, what a delightful surprise! Do, please, come and sit down."

Cecilia remained where she was, twisting her hands together in front of her as she faced him. "A surprise, perhaps, but not a delightful one." Incurably forthright, she went straight to the point while she still had the courage to do so. In his presence, the anger that had fueled her during the walk from Golden Square to Curzon Street was fast ebbing away, and if she did not act quickly, she would never be able to say what she had come to say.

"How *could* you?" she burst out. It was not the cold, relentless cataloguing of his betrayal that she had planned, but when she had gone over and over her speech in the privacy of her bedchamber during the sleepless hours of the previous night, she had not been faced by a man who smiled at her as though she were the greatest treasure in his universe.

"How could I? How could I not do my best to help a friend in trouble? Cecilia, I would do anything for you. How could I stand by and let your life be tied to the life of someone so despicable that his path never should have crossed yours in the first place?"

"It was not your problem to solve. It was mine. And it is not your life. It is my life—a life that would have been a great deal better if you had never come into it."

"How can you say such a thing?" The blood drained from his face, and he looked as though she had struck him. His eyes became dark holes, the skin stretched tight over the high cheekbones. But instead of exulting in the hurt she had managed to inflict on him, Cecilia suddenly found herself awash in the misery of it all.

Drawing a ragged breath and every ounce of strength that remained in her body, she continued. "If you had not ruined us in the first place, Melmouth and his foul bargains would never have entered our lives at all. How could you do it? How could you lead a man to his destruction when your very own father . . . oh, I hate you! I hate you! I hate you!"

To Cecilia's horror, tears began to pour down her cheeks. And he stood there, gazing at her impassively, an unreadable expression in his eyes, his face rigid and inscrutable.

Driven to desperation, she raised her hands and beat them against his chest. "You monster of—"

He caught hold of her wrists, whipping them behind her back where one hand held them in a grip of iron while the other tilted her chin, forcing her to look up at him, to look deep into eyes that were now shadowed with pain.

"Cecilia, listen to me. I never meant to deceive you. When I first met you, I did not immediately realize that you were Shelburne's daughter. Quite simply, you were the angel in my picture, my muse, my companion. It was stupid of me, of course, but I was so happy to have discovered you, to know that the woman, the companion of my dreams was real, that I thought of nothing else.

"It was not until much later that it dawned on me who you were, and by then—God forgive me for being such a coward—I had come to enjoy your company so much that I could not bear the thought of losing you. I know it was wrong. I should have told you the moment I realized.

"But believe me, Cecilia, I did not destroy your father. I did not even ruin him. He was a ruined man before I ever encountered him."

An inarticulate cry of agony and protest rose in Cecilia's chest, but her throat was too tight with pain and tears for it to escape.

"When I looked into your father's eyes that first night at Brooks's I knew there was nothing I could do to stop him, nothing I could do to save him. Other gamblers' eyes are alight with the thrill of the game—the challenge and the risk of it all; either that, or they shine, as my father's did with the fever of it, a fever that can never be assuaged or satisfied. Your father's eyes were empty, lifeless. There was no glow in them, there was no fever, just the hollow depths of hopelessness. He was already lost when he came into my life."

She did not want to listen, did not want to hear him point out what she had known all along. Her father's death had begun the day her mother had died. Young as she was, Cecilia had sensed it. He was loving and caring to the two children left to him to look after for, but the light and the laughter had gone out of his life when she died.

For their sakes, hers and Neville's, he had gone on—

gone to Italy, following his love for art and beauty, surrounded himself with friends who shared that love, and
made a life for them away from the memories of his dead
wife. He had even entered into his daughter's life with all
the pride and enthusiasm of a devoted parent, sharing her
successes with her, comforting her in her frustrations, helping her to learn and grow. But the ebullient man he had
once been so long ago was gone. He had been able to take
pleasure in their beautiful surroundings, to gratify his
senses with the flowers, the food, the wine, and the sunshine, but he had never been truly happy after his wife died.

And then they had had to leave Naples, and he had shriv-
eled up before her very eyes—not physically so much as
emotionally and spiritually. He was still her tall, handsome,
clever father, but there was a sadness about him, an emptiness that even she had not been able to fill.

But Cecilia was not about to admit all that to herself,
much less to the man who had brought it all down around
her—her father, her life, and now her dreams. Angrily, she
shook her head. *No! No! No!* a voice screamed inside of
her.

"Cecilia, you *must* believe me." Sebastian's voice was
desperate now, begging her, willing her to trust in him, but
she remained as if frozen in stone beyond his reach, beyond
all caring.

"We fell into conversation one night at Brooks's. I do not
even remember how it happened. He was an intelligent,
thoughtful man who had but recently come from the Continent, and I was eager to learn firsthand what was happening there. He invited me to a game of piquet from which I
emerged a winner. The next time, knowing how easily I had
won, I declined his invitation. But he insisted, and it
seemed paltry on my part to refuse. I had no idea of his situation, and it seemed churlish to deny a man the entertainment he so earnestly solicited.

"But he kept asking me to play, and he kept losing.
When I remonstrated with him, he responded that I, at least,

offered him intelligent conversation while he was losing, and that, as a connoisseur, he could not bear to lose except to the very best. Who was I to argue with the man?"

Sebastian read the question in her eyes. "No, he was not in the grip of the gambling fever the way my father was, for he suffered no illusions about his chances of winning against me, nor did he seek to repair his fortunes by more risky wagers. He was not, as so many are, driven by greed, but driven by despair. And who was I to sit in judgment on his despair?"

"But you did judge him." At last she managed to get the words out. "You knew he was facing ruin, and you did nothing to stop him." The hurt, the loss, the betrayal welled up inside of her and she could not go on.

"Cecilia, he was as bent on his own destruction as you are on being independent. To deny him would have been to deny him the little dignity he had left in life. The choice was of his own making; it was the choice of his own destiny, his own life. What would you have had me do, refuse him and let him become a victim to someone like Melmouth?"

"No." It was the faintest of whispers, and she would not look him in the eye, but it was an admission, nonetheless.

Relief flooded his heart. She might never admit it to him, but she knew what he said was true.

"Cecilia." Sebastian drew her into his arms and held her tightly, willing himself to drain away some of her pain and sadness.

But it was no use. She remained there motionless for only a moment or two before wrenching herself away. "But that does not absolve you of the guilt you bear for betraying my trust in you, not once, but three times. First, by your not telling me about my father, and second, by not telling me about owning my portrait. I can do nothing about either of those. But the third—your high-handed interference in my affairs without my permission—I can and will do something about. It may take me years to repay you, but I will do it if it takes me the rest of my days. And I will begin with the paintings in your ballroom. I shall complete them, and they will not cost you a single penny. They have, however, already cost you our friendship, and all hope of ever speaking to me again."

And before she could lose the resolve bred by righteous indignation, Cecilia hurried from the room.

Chapter 24

Cecilia had been right to fear that her anger would not last, for she had barely gained the street when such a corroding sense of loss and despair washed over her that she was forced to grab hold of the slim iron railings outside of the Earl of Charrington's town house for support.

The railings dug into her gloved hand as she clung for dear life, her vision blurred with tears that she refused to let fall, her breath coming in painful gasps. It seemed that she clung to the railing forever, willing herself to take a step forward, away from the loss and the pain, to put it all behind her and carry on as though Sebastian, Earl of Charrington, had never entered her life, never brought her the comfort of friendship and understanding, never introduced her to the exquisite happiness of being irresistibly drawn to another human being.

How she made it back to Golden Square, she never knew. She only knew that placing one foot in front of the other, again and again, took an act of courage that she never knew she possessed. All she really wanted to do was to remain clinging to the railings in front of his house, and weep until she was too exhausted to do anything but sleep.

Sleep was what she longed for—the sleep of utter and

total oblivion—when she at last climbed the stairs to her bedchamber.

But such peace was not to be hers. No matter how Susan bathed her aching brow with lavender water, or carried up draughts of chamomile tea, nothing could bring her the peace or unconsciousness she craved.

At last, admitting defeat, Cecilia rose and went down to her studio, hoping against hope that if she could not achieve forgetfulness, she could at least find distraction. But no distraction came. Every stroke of her pencil in her sketchbook reminded her of the ballroom in Grosvenor Square and the man for whom she was creating the pictures—reminded her of waltzing in his arms, looking into his eyes, and knowing that somehow, in spite of his being engaged to marry another woman, she, Cecilia Manners, belonged there.

With a cry of anguish, Cecilia threw down the pencil in despair and dropped her head into her hands. How could this be happening to her, the woman who had so proudly rejected all thought of love and marriage in order to be able to devote herself to her art? Let the others who craved such things suffer the pangs of unrequited affection and desire; she did not deserve it, had never sought it out, had never wanted it in the first place.

Sighing, Cecilia at last raised her head and looked around her studio at her books and her paints, her antique vases and shards of mosaic from Pompeii. Slowly, painfully, she reached under the sofa to retrieve her pencil. She should be grateful to Sebastian for his betrayal, not angry at him: By destroying her trust in him, he had set her free from a dangerous attraction that had threatened to take over her life and her work.

Now he had released her from the spell he had cast over her. She was once again her own independent self: cool, unattached, unaffected, with nothing to do but work to make herself the most important artist in the Royal Academy. And there was no time like the present to set herself back on that path.

She would put aside the pictures for the ballroom, just for the moment, and begin a picture of her own, just for her, the picture she had wanted to do for so long, but had been afraid to start—the prisoner Samson breaking down the pillars in the house of the Philistines.

Slowly, tentatively, Cecilia began to draw, willing her mind to empty itself of everything but the picture before her. Then, faster and faster, with growing assurance, her fingers took over; the swift, rhythmic motion of her hands gradually soothed the ache in her heart and the emptiness in her soul. At last, she was completely immersed in her work—so immersed that she was not even aware of Susan creeping in to light the candles or place a tray of food on the table beside her, so immersed that she would have worked until she dropped, had not Neville appeared in the doorway hours later fussing impatiently.

"What ever are you doing, Cecy? You are not even dressed."

"Dressed?" Dragging her eyes from the sketch before her, she goggled blankly at her brother.

"For the opera. Tonight is the night we are joining the Lievens at the opera." He stared at her incredulously. "Even you could not forget a thing like that? You always enjoy the opera."

"Oh my! Oh dear! Sorry. I shan't be a moment." Hastily shutting her sketchbook, she scurried to her bedchamber where Susan hurried her into her pink satin frock, and did her best to tidy her mistress's hair, clustering the curls around her forehead and coiling it smoothly in the back.

Cecilia reappeared not a quarter of an hour later looking charmingly presentable, though not so exquisitely à la mode as her brother could have wished.

All the way to the opera, she did her best to compose herself, knowing full well that the sharp eyes of Dorothea Lieven, which missed nothing and no one, would notice immediately if she appeared to be the least bit indisposed. But fortunately for Cecilia's peace of mind, they arrived at the beginning of the first act, and the countess was far too distracted by the presence of more noteworthy members of the *ton* to pay much attention to her guests, beyond acknowledging their appearance.

Countess Lieven might be distracted by the wide variety of members of the beau monde who saw fit to show themselves at the opera that evening, but poor Cecilia was not so lucky. There were not a great many members of the *ton* whom she recognized, and far fewer in whom she evinced the slightest interest, so it was not surprising that the first familiar face her wandering gaze encountered as she entered the Lievens' box was that of the Earl of Charrington, who was seated directly opposite them, so that there was absolutely no avoiding seeing him or being seen by him.

Seated next to him, his fiancée was her customary picture of elegance in a gown far more becoming and à la mode than Cecilia's. Her rich dark hair was parted in the latest Parisian style. Susan had enthusiastically described to Cecilia the style earlier that evening, when she had begged her mistress to allow her to dress her hair in a manner that was more fashionable than Cecilia's customary coiffeur.

Fiercely dismissing these lowering observations as the evil product of an unoccupied mind, Cecilia immediately focused her attention on the stage, as the four settled into the box. Soon, blessedly enough, she was lost in the drama of the story and the beauty of the music.

Not so the gentleman opposite her. Far from being able to forget himself in the magnificence of Mozart's score or Metastasio's libretto, Sebastian—wedged in between his fiancée on one side and her great-aunt Letitia, who served as her erstwhile and utterly powerless chaperone on the other—was forced to endure a running commentary on every member of the Upper Ten Thousand who had happened to attend this particular performance, as well as the idiosyncrasies or downright defects of the costumes they had chosen to wear.

For a little while, Sebastian had been naive enough to

imagine that this trivial chatter would cease the moment the music began. He was soon disabused of that ridiculous notion, when there was an insistent *psst* in his ear just as the overture was beginning, as Barbara announced that the Duchess of Rokehampton's gown was at least three years old.

Realizing that by focusing his attention on the stage, he was simply inviting interruptions from his fair companion, Sebastian allowed his gaze to wander idly over the boxes just as Barbara's was doing.

It was then that he saw her. And, having seen her, he wondered how he could have missed seeing her in the first place. That expressive face, vibrant and electrified by the music and drama taking place onstage stood out among all the bored, expressionless countenances surrounding it. How he longed to be near her, to watch the story unfold through her eyes, see them catch fire with the idealistic tale of the legendary emperor, and watch her lips part in exquisite enjoyment of Mozart's ineffable music. Instead he was trapped alone in his box with a shallow, self-centered beauty and her stolidly silent companion.

And thus it would be for the rest of his life. What had he done? What prison of banality and mediocrity had he condemned himself to, all in the name of friendship and gratitude, all in the comfortable belief that there was no such thing as love?

But there *was* such a thing as love. He knew that now. It was sitting across from him in Countess Lieven's box at the opera. And he had destroyed that too, along with the trust that Cecilia had had in him.

What a fool he had been ever to contemplate marriage to a woman like Barbara, ever to think that all one needed was the most distant of relationships to make a marriage—the more distant, the better.

How could he, who had entrusted his most intimate thoughts to a picture for all these years, imagine that he would be satisfied with someone who had less interest in

him than a sympathetic-looking oil painting? At least the
girl in the painting had always listened, had never been
patently bored or uninterested in anything that did not directly revolve around her, which was more than could be
said of his fiancée.

And now, in addition to having irrevocably alienated the
original, he no longer even had his picture for consolation.
Sebastian sighed inwardly. At least he should be grateful to
Barbara for unwittingly proving it to him that he was in love
with Cecilia, and had been from the moment he had seen her
picture. He had just not known what to call that special feeling, but now he did. It was called love.

Now having discovered that he was in love, he should be
equally grateful to Cecilia for having ended it before it had
even started, before he was forced to overcome the urge to
tell her that she was the light, the hope, the comfort, and the
love of his life. For how could he in all honor have told her
that when he had pledged his word to Barbara?

No, it was far better to have it end this way. This way, he
would not be forced to live a lie, because he had never told
her the truth—that he did believe in love, but had simply
never dared to hope that it could actually exist for him. And
now that he knew it did, well, he would just have to forget
he had ever known it. He would have to bury himself even
deeper in his work.

After all, he had lost everything once before and recovered: his home, his father, his mother, his good name. But
this time, he would be starting all over with nothing particular to look forward to, except the gray banality of endless
years stretching before him with Barbara.

Chapter 25

Sebastian was not the only one looking forward to an empty future without the alleviating presence of either color or life—an existence devoid of energy or hope. Cecilia awoke the next morning to the patter of rain drops upon the window and a thick gray fog that hung around her as shapeless, cloying, and impenetrable as her future.

She had no reason to go out, no reason to go anywhere at all, so she remained immured in her studio the entire day, not seeing or talking to anyone, burying herself in her work—or trying to—taking her meals on a tray, and only looking up from her sketching from time to time to take the odd bite of food.

She was so wrapped up in her own misery that she did not notice that Neville was leaving her quite alone. Usually he felt compelled to interrupt her work for one reason or another, whether it was to show off the latest way of arranging his cravat or taking snuff, or to badger her to leave off her work for awhile and behave like a proper gentlewoman.

In fact, in the days that ensued—each one following the next in endless, tedious succession, with nothing in particular to distinguish one from the other, and with nothing in particular to look forward to except more of the same—

Neville was to be seen even less than usual around the house in Golden Square.

While it was true that he spent most of his days among the crowd at Tattersall's, or in the more select company of the clubs along St. James's or strolling down Bond Street, or among the press of carriages thronging Hyde Park at the fashionable hour, he did return home on a regular basis in between these appearances to refresh or to change his attire.

But even his valet admitted, when questioned, that milord had been away from the premises a great deal as of late, which had given the estimable Hudson enough time to take a complete inventory of all his master's cravats, shirts, and pocket handkerchiefs and order replacements for those that would not stand up to his lordship's exacting scrutiny.

Too immersed in her own private despair to pay a great deal of attention to the erratic comings and goings of her brother, Cecilia remained unaware of this change in routine, until it slowly occurred to her that his absences evidenced more than just his usual peripatetic behavior. He was, in fact, around a great deal less than he ever had been before.

When she did eventually cross paths with him in the hall one evening, he wore the expression of someone with something of importance on his mind.

Since Neville never had anything of importance on his mind, this struck his sister as being highly unusual. Her suspicions thoroughly aroused, and her senses already on edge after Neville's disastrous escapade with Lord Melmouth, Cecilia vowed to put aside her own concerns for a little while—at least until she had gotten to the bottom of whatever was consuming so much of her brother's time and attention.

It did not appear to be gambling, for on more evenings than not, he went out attired in evening clothes, and the few breakfast conversations they did share were peppered with references to the Duchess of Wentworth's rout or Lady Hailsham's ridotto, the Countess of Roxburgh's ball and the like. And during the day, according to the bills from the livery stable, he seemed to be hiring a carriage with great regularity.

Fiercely protective of her own independence, Cecilia did not like to pry into her brother's affairs either by posing questions to him directly or, worse yet, questioning the servants—but there was nothing further to be gleaned by simple observation. When she eventually did steel herself to ask him one morning if all were quite well with him, he simply looked at her in surprise. "Yes, quite well, with the natural exception of having one's pockets eternally to let. But we have Papa, among others, to thank for that. Why do you ask? Surely you are not worrying about Melmouth again? I am awake on every suit now, you know; I would not make such a fool of myself twice. I promise you."

But after he had answered her question, he fell silent for such a long time, folding and unfolding his serviette in such an uncustomary fit of abstraction, that his sister remained unconvinced by his reassurances, in spite of his vehemence.

Cecilia told herself that there was little she could do except watch and wait, but somehow that seemed rather poor-spirited, not to mention ineffectual. However, she had no experience in such things. Undoubtedly, someone like the Earl of Charrington, who was accustomed to making his way in the world, would address the issue far more forcefully. But she was not going to think of the Earl of Charrington now. It had been bad enough seeing him at the opera, and though she had mostly succeeded in losing herself in the music, she had not succeeded in doing it to the point that she was not aware of his fiancée's constant chatter or his obviously growing frustration with it.

Cecilia should have taken a great deal of satisfaction from thinking that a man who had destroyed her peace of mind was going to have his slowly eroded away over the years by a wife who continually demanded his attention. Instead, it made her sad to think of an energetic and clever mind doomed to boredom, and wasting away in the company of a woman who clearly had no use for intelligent conversation, if her idle gossip could even be called conversation.

Cecilia's frustration with her own inaction, however, was extremely short-lived, for the very next day her infrequently present brother did not even appear at the breakfast table. However little Neville participated in the rest of his sister's life, he could always be counted on to appear at breakfast, if for no other reason than to badger her for funds. Too undisciplined to pay attention to such a paltry thing as money, he had abdicated all the accounting—both their meager income, and most definitely their expenses—to his sister, who, in addition to paying the tradesmen, looked after the rents from Shelburne Hall and the tenants on their estate.

Neville's absence galvanized her into action. She rang immediately for Tredlow, who somberly denied all knowledge of anything out of the ordinary where his lordship was concerned. But then Tredlow, who had subtly, but pointedly, made it known that he disapproved of his master's self-indulgent life, was hardly the person to possess any useful information about Neville or his whereabouts.

Sedley, however, who worshiped his master's sartorial expertise and his decided air of fashion, was far more forthcoming. "I believe his lordship has gone to visit friends in the country, my lady," he volunteered when Cecilia questioned him.

"And yet you did not see fit to inform her ladyship of this interesting fact?" asked Tredlow, whose thunderous expression boded ill for the hapless footman.

"But I thought she knew," the unfortunate man cast a look of desperate appeal in Cecilia's direction.

"Do not fret, Sedley." Cecilia sighed. "It is not your fault. Please go find Hudson for me, unless he too has gone to the country."

"Oh no, my lady. He is most definitely here, my lady. I shall go and fetch him directly." Happy to be released from the butler's critical presence, Sedley hurried off in search of Neville's valet.

And why am I not reassured by that piece of information? Cecilia asked herself as she waited for Hudson to appear.

The valet was as in the dark as the rest of them with regard to Neville's whereabouts, though he was able to furnish Cecilia with the details of what he had packed in his master's valise.

"And you did not think it odd that the master was not taking you along on this journey? And, even if you did not think it odd, it did not occur to you to mention it to my lady?" The butler's face was positively wrathful.

"Never mind, Tredlow," Cecilia injected in a placating voice. "I know that you mean well, and it is all rather out of the ordinary, but it is not the fault of these gentlemen that we do not know my brother's comings and goings. He is a grown man, after all, with a perfect right to indulge in whatever queer start he wishes to indulge himself in."

The butler's derisive snort, though hastily suppressed, made it clear that he was not about to accord the latitude to his lordship that his ladyship did.

"And that is just what it is; a queer start, and nothing more." Cecilia looked significantly at all three of them. "I thank you for clearing it up for me."

But when they had left, she remained frowning thoughtfully at nothing in particular. Then, resolutely pushing her chair back from the table, she made a decision. "There is nothing for it but to pay a call on Miss Wyatt, unfashionably early though it may be," she remarked to no one in particular.

As she put on her bonnet and pelisse, however, she thought better of it. She could not just call on a woman with whom she was barely acquainted, at what was—in London at least—the very crack of dawn. Possessing herself with as much patience as she could muster, she sent a note around to Russell Square, informing Miss Wyatt that she would call on her in a few hours' time with a few final questions about the choice of frame for the lady's completed portrait.

But when Cecilia arrived later that morning in Russell

Square, she was greeted with the news that Miss Wyatt was not at home.

"Then would you be so good as to give her my card and ask her to call upon me at her earliest convenience. It is a matter of some urgency," Cecilia insisted.

The butler, a far less imposing individual than Tredlow, and not particularly accustomed to dealing with titled females who carried themselves with an air of proud assurance, unbent so far as to confide to Miss Wyatt's visitor that, though the young lady would undoubtedly be most sorry to miss her call, it was unlikely that she would be able to return the favor any time soon, having left not an hour ago to visit a sick aunt in the country.

That was all Cecilia needed to hear to confirm her worst fears. Neville had eloped with the Earl of Charrington's fiancée, and it was all her fault for not having put an end to the affair in the first place, or at least expressed her misgivings to the earl and let him deal with the situation himself.

Now she was in the unenviable position of being forced to call upon a man to whom she had vowed never to speak again, a man whose very existence had caused her no end of misery and soul-searching.

And why that fact should suddenly make her feel more energetic and hopeful, more excited and alive than she had felt in weeks, was something that Cecilia was not at all prepared to think about, much less deal with.

Chapter 26

But deal with it she must—and the sooner the better, if the irresponsible Barbara and Neville were to be saved from their to foolish and ruinous actions. Time was of the very essence, for the story was bound to leak out sooner rather than later—and once the story came out, there would be nothing that Cecilia or Sebastian could do to save Barbara's and Neville's reputations, except to prove beyond a shadow of a doubt that the story was nothing more than a fierce and vicious rumor.

Not even bothering to return to Golden Square, Cecilia took a hackney directly to Curzon Street, where, to her infinite relief, she was admitted immediately and led to the library where she found Sebastian in his shirtsleeves poring over sheaves of what appeared to be financial reports and balance sheets.

For a moment, as she stood in the doorway, Cecilia told herself that she was mad to have come—madder still to think that he would even listen to a woman who not long ago had told him she hated him, and accused him of ruining her father's life as well as her own. But as she hesitated, he looked up, and his smile, when he first saw her standing there—even though it was immediately replaced by a more guarded expression—was all the reassurance she needed.

Sebastian would know what to do. He would help her. In spite of what Neville had said, he was a man of his word—a gentleman who could be trusted to act honorably no matter what it cost him.

"Lady Cecilia." He was instantly aware of the signs of strain in her face, the pallor of her complexion, the eyes that had turned to deep emerald instead of the usual warm hazel, the compressed lips, and the hands clenched tightly in front of her.

He was at her side in a second. "Please sit down and tell me what is troubling you."

Relief flooded through her. She should have known he would recognize her distress the moment she entered the room and do his best to help her.

Cecilia bit her lip, not knowing quite where to begin. "It is all my fault. If I had been paying more attention—if I had spoken to Neville at the very outset—if I had stopped to think, or even mention it to you, this might never have happened."

"What might never have happened?"

"Neville and Barbara."

His blank expression was ample proof that she was being utterly and completely obtuse. "I beg your pardon. I am carrying on like a rattlepate when time is wasting." Cecilia drew a deep steadying breath. "I am very much afraid that Neville and Barbara have eloped. Or, that is to say, I believe they have eloped."

"Ah." It spoke volumes for Sebastian's trust in her that he accepted her opinion without question. "And what have you discovered thus far?"

She smiled gratefully at him. Most people—most men in particular—would have called her all sorts of a hysterical fool, but not Sebastian. He went straight for the facts. "Only that Neville is on some errand so important, so critical to his welfare that he has missed breakfast for the first time in as long as I can remember. And after some questioning, his valet and the footman have volunteered that he has gone to visit a friend in the country—a plan that neither the butler nor I knew anything about. A plan that is ludicrous, considering my brother's penchant, even compulsion, for being in London and nowhere else but London during the Season. Miss Wyatt, it also appears, has been called away to the country, in her case, to administer to an ailing aunt."

"An ailing aunt? Why she has dozens of cousins who live closer than she to the only aunt she possesses, who is also widely recognized as being a hypochondriac of the worst sort. And, having put two and two together, have you also come up with a theory for their eventual destination?"

"No." Cecilia admitted apologetically. "Having been responsible for this much delay, I felt it incumbent upon me to inform you as quickly as possible, so I have not had any opportunity for further research. I am so sorry. It is all my fault. I was worried that something like this might be happening, and I did nothing to stop it. I should have said *something,* done *something.*" She twisted her gloved hands together. "If only I had, then none of this would have happened."

Sebastian took both her hands in a comforting grasp. "My dear girl, do not take on so. How could you possibly have known or even guessed such a thing?"

"I saw how they were—laughing and flirting with one another—and I did nothing."

"Do not be so hard on yourself. Barbara is a beautiful woman and a natural-born coquette. She would act that way toward any admiring gentleman, whether she was planning to elope with him or not. And Neville would play the admiring gallant to any beautiful, fashionable woman, no matter who she was."

This bracing observation drew a reluctant nod from Cecilia. "Perhaps. But I still think that I am right and that we must do what we can to stop them, and quickly."

The earl was silent for so long that she could not help looking up at him curiously, only to discover him gazing down at her intently with the oddest glow in his dark eyes.

"I agree with you wholeheartedly. We will go after them, and we will rescue them from their own stupidity, but not before I tell you, Cecilia how very sorry I am about your father. How sorry I am that I did not save him from himself. How sorry I am that I allowed demons of my own past to ruin your future. I should have realized that in ignoring your father's plight I was punishing my own for not being strong enough to resist the lure of the gaming table. I told myself that it was different with your father—that he courted his own destruction while mine was too blind, too ignorant even to recognize that his was coming. There is nothing I can say, nothing I can do to make that up to you, Cecilia, but that does not mean that I will ever stop trying to do so.

"And now," he reached down to take one of her clenched hands in his and raise it to his lips, "having suffered for my moral cowardice toward your father, you have come to do your best to save my honor and the honor of my fiancée. I do not know that I deserve such consideration from you, but I bless you for having given it to me." And turning her hand over in his, he pressed his lips into her palm.

Again Cecilia felt as though an electric shock had run through her, and life once again seemed to flow back in to her veins. How well he understood her! How quickly he seemed to know, without her even voicing it, that it was her concern for his happiness, not Neville and Barbara's, that had driven her back on her vow never to speak to him again. How acutely he sensed what it must be costing her to do so. He not only recognized it, but he was generous enough to appreciate it and accept her help. The least she could do was to accept in the same generous spirit his explanation of what had occurred with her father. "Thank you," she whispered.

"And now, my own personal Bow Street Runner, having solved the mystery of my fiancée's and your brother's trips to the country, do you have any suggestions as to where the two of them might possibly be headed in such a precipitate manner?"

"Gretna Green?"

He shook his head. "Far too uncomfortable. Barbara would never attempt such a journey without trunks full of clothes, carriages full of servants, and outriders to smooth her path the entire way."

"The ailing aunt?"

"Far too unfashionable. The aunt, her dead mother's sister, was married to a village shopkeeper and sired numerous offspring before giving in to the numerous ailments that keep them all dancing attendance on her—a retribution she undoubtedly exacts for having successfully succeeded in shepherding six sickly and demanding infants safely into adulthood. She lives in some obscure village miles from any good-sized metropolis or even a main road. No, it is highly unlikely that Barbara considered going there even for a moment. It must be somewhere else, but where?"

"The livery stable!"

"Where?"

"No. I mean that Neville must have used the carriage from the livery stable. Undoubtedly they will be able to tell us at least the general direction in which he was headed."

"Clever girl. Let us go there at once."

It was one thing, however to identify a possible source of information, and quite another to elicit that information without giving rise to suspicions that would inevitably lead to further gossip.

It was Sebastian who solved this problem by sauntering in to the stable and in his most toplofty manner observed disdainfully to his companion, "Clearly there is nothing here for us in this establishment."

"Now see here, governor, you have no call to speak that way. This here is a first-rate stable here, this is," one of the grooms replied, taking instant exception to Sebastian's disapproval.

"How can it be when I see only hacks, and no post-horses capable of making it as far as Kensington, much less Weybridge or Barnet."

"And that shows how much you know, my dear sir. Why

not an hour and a half ago we dispatched a most well-appointed coach and four to Hounslow and they should be there in well under the usual time."

"And all that will not do me any good, will it now, my man—for what earthly good to me is a coach and four bound for Hounslow when I need one for Barnet?" And turning on his heel, Sebastian walked briskly back towards Cecilia.

"They are headed to Hounslow," he told her cheerfully, "which means that we should not have too much difficulty catching up to them, especially if we have some idea of their ultimate destination."

"Oh, we know that well enough now," she responded grimly. "Shelburne Hall. Neville is headed to Shelburne. Of course! What a ninny I am. I should have thought of that before. He will prevail upon the vicar there to marry them. After all, the living is at Neville's disposal, even though we have rented it to tenants. The vicar, who has known him since he was a boy, would be a fool to risk upsetting him, even if he wanted to. But he would not. The Reverend Dr. Cuthbert Adams is the world's most trusting creature. It would simply never occur to him to question anything Neville might ask for."

"Then it is to Shelburne I must go, if you but give me the directions."

"*We* will go."

"Now see here, my girl, it is not that I do not appreciate your concern, and I thank you for establishing the fugitives' whereabouts—which you have done with admirable dispatch—but when it comes to pursuing them, sheer brawn and very little brain is required—sheer brawn and a great deal of speed, which is why I am planning to go after them in my curricle."

"And I plan to accompany you."

"It will be excessively uncomfortable. I shall be driving rather fast, and I do not intend to stop."

"Are there banditti?"

"Are there what?"

"Banditti. Nothing the English roads have to offer can possibly compare to the hopeless tracks that pass for roads in Italy. I am more than accustomed to enduring extended journeys on those roads, and then there is the constant fear of being held up by banditti. So you see, riding in a well-sprung curricle along the Oxford-London road with no threat of banditti does not sound even remotely uncomfortable to me. I promise I will not distract you by talking. Besides, when we catch up to them, my presence will insure that no whisper of scandal is associated with your fiancee's reputation."

Sebastian knew when he was beaten, even without seeing the determined glint in her eye. "Very well then, I shall call for you in Golden Square in half an hour's time. Will you be ready by then?"

They had been walking as they had been talking, and by now they had reached Cecilia's own doorstep. "Of course I shall be ready. I am not such a poor creature that a journey into Oxfordshire, even in a curricle, gives me pause."

Chapter 27

There were others, however, for whom a journey into Oxfordshire, especially in a hired carriage, was the epitome of discomfort. Barbara Wyatt was not used to ill-sprung chaises whose windows rattled, or horses whose pace was a bare six miles an hour even on the flat. "Really, Neville, you should have tried another stable. Surely there is at least one establishment in London capable of producing a decent coach and four."

"But my dear, you found this very vehicle to be quite adequate on what, I believe you called our *delightful drive* to Lady Hambleden's Venetian breakfast in Richmond."

"Then we were not trying to cover miles upon miles of road. At the rate we are going, it will take us an age to reach Shelburne, and I am already quite shaken to pieces."

"Relax, my dear. Respite is in sight. We are just coming to the posting house at Hounslow now. Do bear in mind, however, that you are my sister."

"Yes, Neville." Placated by the thought of a comfortable chair and a restorative meal, Barbara shot him a saucy smile as he helped her down from the carriage.

But the posting house was not to her liking, for the host, though hospitable enough, was not agog with the same admiration that the postboys and the coachman had been. Nor did she find the food anything but barely edible. The soup was cold, the mutton tough, and Barbara very much feared that the fish was not fresh.

Gritting his teeth, Neville took it all in stride, excusing her ill humor as the natural enough result of nerves. After all, it was not every day that a gently bred young lady eloped with a penniless man, marquess though he might be. Taking a deep breath, he smiled encouragingly at her as he rose to escort her back to their carriage. "Never mind, my dear. What is the discomfort of one small journey when you have the rest of a lifetime to be treated like a queen by your most humble servant?"

This brought forth a smile at least. "I do not mean to complain. It is just that I am not accustomed to having to travel in this way."

"No. Nor will you ever have to again, I promise. Now come along, my dear."

"May we not walk in the garden a little while? The air is so deliciously fresh after the stuffiness of the carriage, and I quite ache with having to sit so cramped for so long."

Neville gave her his arm with a flourish and led her toward the hostelry's remarkably fine rose garden, then around the fish pond at the back, until at last she declared herself fit to travel again.

But the horses they had procured at this latest stop were even slower than the previous team, and they lumbered along, making very poor time until they reached the next stop some two hours later.

Meanwhile, Sebastian and Cecilia, burdened by neither a heavy traveling carriage nor livery-stable horses, not to mention the need for fresh air, made excellent time. They rolled into the inn yard at Hounslow not more than an hour after Barbara and Neville had departed, a piece of information unwittingly supplied by the host in response to Sebastian's offhand comment about the quietness of the hostelry.

"Oh no, my lord, it's been a steady stream of business we have had all day long. Why just an hour or so ago a young man and his sister on their way to Oxfordshire dined here—even stopped to admire my wife's roses, they did. And very fine roses they are, I must admit."

"Thus the power of the disparaging remark," Sebastian observed climbing back into the curricle. "The respondent is so ardent in his own defense that he never has the least recollection of having furnished any information at all— whereas a direct question would affront him to the point that he would wonder what business it was of mine to ask it."

"I shall have to remember never to defend myself against your criticisms, lest I find myself divulging valuable information that I do not wish to have known."

He laughed. "Ah no, you are far too clever for that." He cracked his whip over the team's ears, and they left the innyard at a brisk pace, which they maintained for the entire next leg of the journey, Sebastian having tipped the ostler handsomely in order to get the very best horses the stable had to offer.

News of Neville and Barbara's recent departure greeted them at the next inn, and Sebastian reported somewhat reluctantly to his companion that they were definitely gaining on the pair in front of them. "Which is a great pity because I cannot think when I have enjoyed a journey more, or driven with a more accommodating partner than you have been."

The smile that accompanied this accolade turned Cecilia's bones to water as she fought the self-conscious blush that rose to her cheeks despite her best efforts to hide it.

"But then, you are accustomed to long, uncomfortable journeys. Tell me, do you miss Italy as much as you father did?"

"Oh yes, very much." Cecilia could not help giving him credit for not avoiding the vexing subject of her father, and for trying to prove to her that he had not only played cards with him, but had taken the time to learn something about the man as well. "The very air is magical there, warm and filled with the scent of flowers and fruit blossoms. And the ocean—you have never seen a more lovely shade of blue. There is music everywhere, and one cannot help but be inspired by the surrounding beauty. The warmth of the sunshine affects everyone. Many people say that the Neapolitans are lazy, but I think it is simply that they know how to take pleasure in life."

"You make it sound so magical that I long to see it for myself. Now that Europe has been freed from the grip of the Corsican monster, I am anxious to see all those places I have only read about. Before the war, I was too busy studying, and then trying to rebuild the family estate, but now . . . now I should like very much to travel and explore the world."

His voice trailed off and Cecilia knew he was thinking, as she was, that a wife who considered the London Season to be the very pinnacle of happiness—not to mention a wife who was accustomed to spending her days in comfort surrounded by every luxury that money could buy—was hardly likely to share this dream with him.

She was saved, however, from having to make a reply by an unexpected gust of wind and a sudden darkening of the sky, as a cloud loomed ominously ahead of them.

"I am rather afraid that your traveler's mettle is about to be put to the test," Sebastian had barely time to remark before the first heavy drops of rain spattered around them.

For the next few minutes, he was preoccupied with managing his team, that took exception to the passing shower, but it was over as quickly as it had come. By the time he had tightened his grip on the reins and focused all his attention on the road ahead of them, the sun had reappeared.

It was enough, however, to give them both a good wetting, and Cecilia's sarsenet pelisse clung to her uncomfortably. "My poor girl, you must be soaked through. Here, take this." Pulling the team to a halt, Sebastian secured the reins, stripped off his coat, and wrapped it tenderly around Cecilia's shoulders.

She smiled gratefully at him, and all that he could think of was how desperately he wished that it was the two of them who were the eloping couple, not Neville and Barbara. "Cecilia," he began hoarsely.

Her eyes, full of longing and understanding told him all that he needed to know. She was as loath for the journey to end as he was. She too wanted it to continue on forever, just the two of them, talking and sharing the pleasure of the passing scenery, the fresh air, and spring in the countryside, free for the moment from the burdens of their responsibilities.

"Cecilia, let us . . ." But he could not in all honor voice the treacherous thought that haunted him, which was that perhaps the happiest thing for all of them would be to let Neville and Barbara reach Shelburne and carry out their elopement as planned.

"Yes? What is it?" There was a look in Sebastian's eyes that she could not fathom, dark and cloudy, almost as if he were in pain.

He sighed and pulled her to him, his lips coming down hard on hers. It was the only way he could keep himself from saying what was in his heart: that he loved her, that he wanted her desperately, that he longed with every fiber of his being to beg her to be his wife—to share the rest of her life with him, to travel to foreign lands and cultivate interesting friends who conversed intelligently on topics more important and inspiring than fashion and the *haut ton*—to live life the way it should be lived, the way he had longed to live it since he had first seen her picture—with her.

Cecilia's lips parted under his, and she clung to him with a desperation that told him she too longed to forget everything but the two of them.

But the impatient stamping of the horses and the rattling of the harness brought them to their senses.

Gently, sadly, Sebastian released her, and—giving a final tug to wrap his coat more tightly around her shoulders—once again took up the reins. There was nothing more to say or do, but continue on the course they had set for themselves: rescuing two selfishly heedless people from the consequences of their own rash actions.

And so they continued, but they rode in silent sympathy now, each one struggling with desire and duty, and knowing with a sinking feeling that duty always won.

Chapter 28

It was only a few more miles before the next posting house appeared. As they pulled into the yard, ostlers were busy hitching horses to a traveling carriage, and from the anxious looks that the coachman was casting in the general direction of the inn's entrance, it appeared that something somewhere had gone amiss.

The next instant, a lady, exquisitely attired in a green sarsenet pelisse and a bonnet with ribbons and feathers to match, marched out into the yard, furling and unfurling her parasol in agitation. "I cannot go another mile in this rattling bone-breaker, I tell you. I am already shaken half to death," she declared in a petulant voice.

"But think, my dear, it is only an hour or two more at most," her companion pleaded in the conciliating manner of one who had been repeating this refrain for the better part of the day.

"I *will not* go on."

Sebastian pulled his team to a halt in the yard, jumped down from the curricle and strode toward the young woman, after tossing the reins to the ostler who, glad to be away from the scene of unpleasantness, had come hurrying forward with more than his usual alacrity. "You would prefer, then, to spend the night in a country inn? I think not."

"Charrington!" Barbara gasped. "What are you doing here?"

"I would think that is a question better addressed to you. For my part, I am here to save you from what would appear to be a most uncomfortable situation." He then turned his back on the petulant beauty, and strode around to help Cecilia alight, smiling at her encouragingly before turning back to his fiancée. "Now if you will leave off complaining, I think we had all better go inside and sort out this entirely unnecessary situation."

Barbara gaped at her husband-to-be as though she were seeing him for the very first time. Heretofore, the Earl of Charrington had been nothing more to her than a mere convenience, a voucher to Almack's, a title and a family that would insure her a premier position in the *ton*, and go a long way toward establishing her as a leader in the fashionable world. Lately, of course, he had also come to represent an impediment to her amusement, and an escort whose absence kept her from attending the functions she wished to attend in the style in which she wished to attend them. But, whatever else he had been, he had never, until this moment, existed for her as a person. Now hearing the annoyance in his voice and reading the scorn in his eyes, it struck her with shattering clarity that this was a man whose patience had been severely tried, a man whose wife-to-be was in a compromising situation from which he was forced to extricate her. And he did not look the least bit happy about it.

It was a totally new experience for Barbara, and she had not the least notion how to respond, but she knew that she suddenly felt more tired and wretched than she could ever remember having felt, and at this moment her fiancé, no matter how irritated he might be, looked like a man who was going to remedy that situation for her. "Very well," she replied meekly and headed back toward the inn.

"Cecy?"

"Don't bother, Neville." And turning on her heel, Cecilia trooped tiredly after Miss Wyatt.

Within minutes, Sebastian had requested a private parlor

and refreshment and ordered the inn's own post chaise to be prepared for a return journey to London. While it might not compare in luxury or comfort to the carriages in which Barbara was accustomed to traveling, it was new enough that its windows did not rattle, and it was far better sprung than the equipage that had brought Neville and Barbara from London.

While the landlord was busy ordering refreshments and conveyances for this ill assorted party, Sebastian was holding forth in the parlor. He turned to his fiancée and Neville. "What I find absolutely incredible is that the two of you—who have more than once accused both Lady Cecilia and me of being totally oblivious to the dictates of the *ton*, which you say one ignores to one's peril—should be so dead to all sense of propriety that you would not realize that an escapade such as this would place you utterly beyond the pale of good society. Such a calamity, as you well know, would not cause someone like me or Lady Cecilia to lose a moment's sleep, but to two people such as you, it would be worse than ruin—not to mention completely incomprehensible—which is why Lady Cecilia and I cannot allow you to do this to yourselves, no matter what your motives."

The Earl of Charrington drew a deep breath and continued. "Now I have contrived to locate a slightly more commodious conveyance than the one you employed to come here to take you back to London and, as Lady Cecilia has endured an even more uncomfortable journey than you have"—he shot a quelling glance at his fiancée—"I would suggest that you and she, along with Neville, take your places in that carriage and return to London with all possible speed. I shall be following you in my curricle."

There was nothing more to be said. By now, any member of the party who might possibly have objected was too exhausted and dispirited to do anything but comply with what now, in the cold, clear light of recent experience, seemed to be the most reasonable solution.

So it was that as the sun was slowly sinking in the west,

Barbara, Neville, and Cecilia climbed into the carriage and settled in for the long and tedious trip back to the metropolis.

Of the subdued little group, only Barbara was not too exhausted to comment acidly that the new carriage was hardly an improvement over the old.

Cecilia did not deign to offer a reply to such a useless observation. Her brother, however, addressed Barbara in cajoling tones. "One must look on the bright side: at least it is a different carriage, and therefore we are likely to be bruised in different places than we were in the first vehicle. And Charrington is quite right, you know. Uncomfortable as it is, it is far better to endure a few more hours in this carriage than a night at that inn. Besides, no one looking for scandal could have cause to remark on a day trip to the country in the company of your fiancé and my sister. A night, however, would be a great deal more difficult to explain."

An infuriated sniff was all the response he received to his valiant attempts to placate her.

And for the rest of the journey home, Cecilia could not help but wonder how a man like Sebastian, who had such an appreciation for a cheerful and conversational traveling companion, was going to be able to endure a lifetime full of trivial chatter and continuous demands. How could he, in spite of what he felt he owed to Sir Richard Wyatt, have offered himself up to such an iniquitous bargain?

If the truth be told, Sebastian—keeping his eyes fixed on the carriage in front of him, and trying to ignore the deepening chill of the evening air—was asking himself the very same question. What on earth had possessed him, and how was he going to bear it, especially now when he knew what true love and companionship were really like?

The one consolation he could take from all of this was that Lady Cecilia Manners, in spite of her feelings about his failure to save her father, could not say that he had not conducted himself in a thoroughly honorable fashion. Sebastian had seen the warmth of approval in her eyes and felt the encouragement in her tired smile as he had addressed them all in the inn parlor that evening. And from that tiny bit of approval he would have to take enough consolation to last a lifetime of loneliness and isolation.

But oh how he wished he had held her in his arms and told her how very much she meant to him—told her that he loved her now and would love her always. No matter how long he lived as Barbara's husband, his heart would be Cecilia's forever, as it had been hers since before he even knew her name, when she was nothing but a picture on his wall.

There was nothing more Sebastian could do except return to London, explain to Sir Richard his daughter's absence as best he could, and marry Barbara with as much pomp and ceremony as her social ambition craved. After that, they would go their separate ways. Odd, how chilling what once had seemed so normal sounded, now that he had met Cecilia and learned the joy of true love.

Once she was properly married, Barbara would probably not complain of his inattention to her, for it would then be perfectly acceptable for her, as a dashing young matron, to have any number of admirers fighting one another for the honor of escorting her to this ball or that ridotto. She, at least, would be relatively content with the situation. For Sebastian, it would be an altogether different matter indeed, but he would just have to bear it as best he could.

How cruel it was that what had once seemed to be such a rational union, so free of the pressure of romantic expectations and emotional pressures now seemed so frighteningly empty and desolate.

But he must not dwell on that. He must think of ways in which he could still help Cecilia achieve her dream. Helping her as best he could, with what little help she would allow him to offer, would form the sum total of his happiness in life. He was not without influence in the City. At the very least, he could insure her a steady stream of commissions for portraits, which, if they did not directly advance her goal of becoming a history painter, would at least relieve her of some of the financial worries brought on by that useless brother of hers.

It was even possible that he could convince her to let him invest some small portion of the commissions she received in a variety of financial instruments, so that she would have some money she could call her own, safe and protected from the depredations of Neville's wilder schemes for raising the wind, like gambling with Lord Melmouth. This vague hope that he might be able to assist her in the future was all that he had left.

Chapter 29

At last, they drew up in front of the house in Golden Square. Neville, opening the door so he could hand his sister out of the carriage, was surprised to discover Sebastian already there, ready to do the very same thing. There was nothing he could do but cast a final encouraging smile at Barbara and follow his sister and the earl.

Gently taking Cecilia's arm, Sebastian led her up the steps and, pausing at the top to take her hand in his, pressed it to his lips. "Thank you," he whispered. "Thank you for everything."

And then he was gone, climbing tiredly back into his curricle as the now diminished entourage headed toward Russell Square.

The kiss had been the formal, if old-fashioned, gesture of respect that gentlemen had once shown ladies in a bygone era, but none of its effect was lost on Neville, who whistled silently to himself as he followed his sister into the house.

Here was a fine kettle of fish. It was now plain as pikestaff that the Earl of Charrington was in love with his sister, and—now that Neville thought back on the special understanding that seemed to exist between the two of them—she was very likely in love with the earl. And there they were, the pair of them too proper and too responsible by far to do anything about it.

Well, he, Neville, Marquess of Shelburne, refused to stand idly by and let the two of them ruin their lives—not to mention two perfectly good fortunes. For once in his life, he was not going to leave it up to others to take charge and sort things out. The very first thing tomorrow he was going to pay a visit to Sir Richard Wyatt and put things to rights.

What a fool he had been all this time, spending his energy trying to get his sister married to a fortune when it was far easier to do it himself. Granted, Miss Wyatt did not have the impeccable antecedents that would ensure her true social cachet, but with her elegant face and figure, his decided air of fashion, and his own illustrious antecedents he would make her a leader of the *ton* in no time. The elopement had been an emotional and poorly conceived notion on Barbara's part. A formal offer of marriage from a peer of the realm whose title and family eclipsed Charrington's was quite another.

Neville was so pleased with himself for having come up with a plan that was even more clever than Barbara's that he went straight upstairs to his bedchamber and fell promptly asleep, worn out by the exertions of the day.

Other members of the party, however, were not so fortunate. After having restored his fiancée to the tender care of her maid, Sebastian was enduring a most uncomfortable interview with her father.

Sir Richard, being the astute man of affairs that he was, was not about to believe any convenient tales of sick relatives. "It is the most utter nonsense. Why, even if Barbara gave a rap for her aunt, which she does not, she would be completely useless in a sickroom, and I hope that a daughter of mine would have the good enough sense to know that at the outset. Now what is all this about, Charrington?"

"I believe it is all my fault, sir, and therefore I must bear most of the blame for this, er, *escapade*. You see, I know that to Barbara, the *ton* and its amusements are the very stuff of life, and I know that I have been far too wrapped up in my own affairs to give her the attention she deserves. Her running away was, I believe, her way of pointing out to me my unfortunate neglect."

The financier sighed heavily. "Your fault, perhaps, but mostly mine. When her mother died, I was also too immersed in my affairs to pay much attention to her, and the nurses and governesses I employed to look after her were no match for my headstrong daughter, who was bent on having her own way. She has always been too much indulged, I fear, and now she rides roughshod over everyone—which is why I was so pleased at having you as a son-in-law, for you are one of the few men I know who is strong enough to stand up to her."

"Thank you, sir. I shall do my best," Sebastian responded wearily. "Now if you will forgive me, sir, it has been rather a long day."

"Yes, of course, my lad. Be off with you. And thank you for saving my daughter from her own willful impulsiveness."

But as he led his visitor to the door, Sir Richard's sharp old eyes saw more than weariness in Sebastian's face. It was more than a long, exhausting drive that had robbed him of his usual energetic stride and proud bearing, and the air of mastery and command that distinguished him from other men. This was something far deeper, almost sorrowful—something that Sir Richard could not quite identify, but it was affecting Sebastian more than anything he had seen in all the years of their friendship.

At last, Sebastian was free to return to his own chambers, where one of his library walls was completely bare; the spot where her portrait had hung was as empty as his heart. All that he had to keep him company now was the memory of the look in her eyes as he had thanked her, and the slight pressure of her fingers as he had kissed her hand.

Did she know how much it had cost him not to leave the other two to their own fate, turn his horses toward the Great

North Road and drive on, not stopping until they reached Gretna Green? Would she ever guess how he had longed to let her brother and his fiancée suffer the consequences of their own foolish actions so that he could spend the rest of his life with the woman he loved—the woman who had made him feel happier than he had ever dreamed possible?

No, she would never truly know how much it had cost him, and he would never tell her. Instead he would spend the rest of his life being the model husband to a woman who did not care to whom she was married, just so long as being married made her a leader in the *ton*.

But Sebastian's desolate picture of the future was not entirely accurate, as Sir Richard Wyatt was to discover the very next morning when the butler announced that there was a visitor to see him.

"A visitor, Radlett?" Sir Richard looked up from his correspondence in some surprise. He was not a particularly sociable man, being far too busy to indulge in such things. Most of his acquaintances were financial men like himself, and were therefore far more likely to seek him out at Garroway's or Lloyd's—or any other of the coffeehouses that catered to men of the City—than they were to call on him in Russell Square.

"Yes, sir. It is a Marquess of Shelburne, sir. He is most insistent, sir. He warned me that his name might not be familiar to you, sir, so he told me to inform you that the purpose of his visit concerns Miss Wyatt's journey to the country yesterday."

A cold fear gripped Sir Richard's heart—a fear that this man had come with compromising information about Barbara that he intended to use to his advantage. Not that Sir Richard cared a farthing for what passed as scandal in the fashionable world; he was a plainspoken man himself, who judged people by what they did and what they had to offer, not by what the rest of the world said about them. But his daughter was a different thing altogether. She cared a great deal for what was said about whom in the beau monde. She wanted to be a leader of the *ton* and, by God, if that was what she wanted, he was not about to let anyone stand in her way, especially not some marquess he had never heard of.

However, the handsome young man who was ushered into the library some moments later did not look like a man bent on blackmail or any other nefarious purpose. He might be a bit too finicky in his mode of dress for Sir Richard's taste, but he had a pleasant, open countenance and a winning, gentlemanly air that was hard to resist.

"I do beg your pardon, Sir Richard, for having the temerity to call upon you without the formality of an introduction, but my business with you is too important to delay," the young man apologized.

Sir Richard eyed him warily. "As you say, my lord, we have no previous acquaintance; therefore, I do find it rather difficult to believe that we have any business together."

"In a manner of speaking we do, though. You see, I owe you something."

"Owe me something?"

"Yes. I owe you and your daughter an apology, sir. You see, yesterday I had the effrontery to elope with your daughter, when really what I should have been doing was asking you for her hand, sir."

"I think we had better sit down, my lord." Sir Richard indicated a chair by the fireplace and took one opposite. "And now perhaps you would like to tell me exactly what you mean."

"It is rather delicate, sir."

"Somehow I think that if you were on the verge of eloping with my daughter, the time for delicacy is long since past."

"Perhaps you are unaware that she was not entirely happy with the choice of her prospective husband, sir."

The silence that greeted this observation was nothing short of deafening.

Unfazed, Neville continued. "She is a charming, vivacious young woman, sir—a young woman for whom gaiety and society are as essential to her as the air she breathes. Her fiancé—though he is a most worthy gentleman indeed—not only does not enjoy such things, he avoids them. She was lonely, sir, lonely and neglected. She felt unsupported in what can be a very critical and unforgiving world. Being shy and unsure of herself in this world, she sought me out for advice."

Though the picture of his daughter as being shy and unsure was an entirely new one to him, Sir Richard did not let on. "Go on."

"As I am considered to be something of an expert in these things, she began to consult me more regularly concerning the ways of the *ton*, and as we gradually became friends, I occasionally offered my escort to her and her great-aunt Letitia for some of the more important functions her fiancé was not able to attend. Over time, she came to rely on me more and more, until one day she confided in me that she was miserable at the thought of being married to a man who cared so little for the things that were important to her, and crucial to her happiness. In short, she begged me to take her away, which, being a gentleman whose code it has always been to serve, I did. I arranged for us to be married by a special license, by the vicar who has faithfully served our family and the parishioners of our estate his entire life."

"And am I to surmise that the only reason you are not yet married to my daughter is that the Earl of Charrington had the temerity to object to his fiancée's running off with another man, and came after you?"

"You are, sir." Neville beamed at him as would a devoted schoolmaster whose favorite student had just made an exceedingly clever remark.

"And why, may I ask, should I even listen to your preposterous proposal, instead of having you thrown out of my house immediately?"

"Because Bar—er, because your daughter will be happier with me, sir, than she would ever be with the Earl of Charrington. We are very much alike, she and I. We like the same things. We know how to enjoy life's pleasures to the fullest and how to amuse others. I will be able to grant her dearest wish, which is to be a diamond of the first water, an Incomparable, a hostess whose every affair is characterized as a sad crush. She will become a leader of the *ton*. And while I do not pretend to have the fortune to offer her that the Earl of Charrington does"—here Neville had the grace to look self-conscious—"my title and my family are far more ancient than his. And the title of Marchioness of Shelburne carries with it a certain cachet that the Countess of Charrington simply does not. Don't you agree?"

But by this time, the financier was too overwhelmed by the sheer audacity of his visitor's proposal to do anything but stare at him.

"I know it is a bit of a facer, sir, but if you do not believe me, perhaps you would like to ask your daughter yourself."

"Thank you," Sir Richard gasped as he rang the bell. "I shall do just that."

"Sir?" The butler, who had been hovering as close to the library door as he dared, materialized instantly.

"Please ask Miss Wyatt to come to the library immediately."

He turned back to Neville. "And now, sir, since, as you admit, we are not acquainted, you will tell me something about yourself before my daughter joins us."

But if the truth were told, Sir Richard hardly heard a word that Neville uttered, for he was far too busy remembering how much happier and more vivacious his daughter had appeared in the last few weeks, and how somber his prospective son-in-law had looked the previous evening. Perhaps he had been too eager for the match between his daughter and the Earl of Charrington, because Sebastian was the closest thing there was to the son he had never had. By marrying him to his daughter he would have made official a relationship that had existed informally for so many years. But in his eagerness to gain Sebastian as a son, he had ignored his daughter and the person she was. Now that he considered it, he realized how different they were from one another. If he had noticed this difference at all, Sir Richard had hoped, as was often the case, that the two would balance one another out and not, as was equally often the case, wind up in a disastrously distant relationship.

"You wanted to see me, Papa?" Barbara appeared in the doorway—a picture, as always, in a charming morning gown of primrose jaconet muslin. "Neville!" She came to a stop the moment she saw him. "What ever are you doing here?"

Her father watched with a great deal of interest as a delicate flush tinged his daughter's cheeks. "Odd as it may seem, my dear, this gentleman has come to ask for your hand in marriage. If what he says is true, it appears that you will be a great deal happier being married to him than you would being married to the Earl of Charrington. Is this true?"

"Well, I . . . that is to say, I do not know . . . I do not know quite what to say." She looked appealingly at Neville.

Neville smiled reassuringly at her. "What you do know is that, except for the uncomfortable journey we just recently undertook, which was purely the fault of a badly sprung carriage, that we always have a bang-up time together."

"That is true."

"And you are always telling me that no one makes you laugh the way I do."

"Charrington never makes me laugh."

"And you can always count on me to tell you honestly if a bonnet is not quite the thing or if the color you have chosen is passé."

"Yes, most definitely, but—"

"And being a marchioness, especially in such an ancient and respected peerage, is a great deal more fun than being a mere countess."

"True. But what will people say? I do not wish to be labeled a jilt."

"You will not be labeled a jilt if you marry someone of

superior rank and lineage. Besides, all you need to say is that you and Charrington simply did not suit, and the world will be well satisfied."

"Then, if you please, Papa," Barbara smiled appealingly at her father, "I would a great deal rather be married to Neville than to Charrington, who is stiff and cold and dull. I know he is wealthy and he is your friend, but you have always said that I am wealthy enough to do what I please. I will have ever so much more fun with Neville."

There was no mistaking the relief in his daughter's eyes. Shaking his head, her father smiled ruefully. "Very well, Puss. You know I never could deny you anything that you wanted, and I am not about to start now. You may marry this man if you wish to. But I warn you, young man," he shook an admonitory finger at Neville, "she will lead you a merry dance."

"And so she has already, sir," his future son-in-law agreed. "So she has already."

Chapter 30

And so it was that later that day, Sebastian, who little more than twenty-four hours earlier had stood in Sir Richard Wyatt's library, promising his prospective father-in-law that he would stand up to his willful daughter, found himself standing in that very same library listening in stunned amazement as that willful daughter broke their engagement, then vowing nobly to Barbara and her father that he would do nothing to stand in the way of her happiness. If he had his doubts about the reliability of her new husband-to-be, he kept silent, as he realized that she truly did look a good deal more animated at the prospect of becoming the Marchioness of Shelburne than she had ever been at the prospect of becoming the Countess of Charrington.

After taking leave of his former fiancée and her father, Sebastian decided to walk home, to clear his head and give him time to adjust to the wide and wonderful vistas that had just opened up before him—to an entire life that was now a future to be looked forward to.

But his day of surprises was far from over, as, a few hours later, he was astounded to learn that the Marquess of Shelburne was awaiting his presence in his very own library.

"Hello, old man." Irrepressible as ever, Neville held out his hand as Sebastian entered the room. "I realize that it may seem a bit outré calling on the man whose fiancée has just left him for oneself, but in this case, I must venture to say that I think it all for the best. Surely, you will agree that the lady and I are far better suited to one another than are the lady and you. There are no hard feelings, I trust?"

"No hard feelings."

"Good. Then we can proceed to the next issue, and the true reason for my visit, which is to tell you that there is someone else who is far better suited to you than Miss Wyatt could ever be: my sister."

"Your sister?"

Neville laughed. "I may not be a clever fellow like you, Charrington, but I've eyes in my head. I have seen the way you two look at one another, heard the way you talk with one another. Cecy is a good girl, but far too serious and responsible by half. I suspect that you are precisely the same, which should take a great deal of the worry off her shoulders — though with my marrying Barbara, a great deal of worry will already have been. Well, I shan't embarrass you any further with my presence, but I just wanted you to know that if you want my blessing to marry Cecy, you may have it. I shall likely be at White's the rest of the day, and she will be at home, so you do not need to fear to put it to the touch."

And with a jaunty wave of his curly-brimmed beaver, the Marquess of Shelburne was gone, leaving Sebastian to stare fixedly at the empty spot on his wall where Cecilia's picture had recently resided.

How long he stood there, he had no idea, until suddenly, coming to his senses, he muttered, "He is right. There is no time like the present." He snatched up his hat and gloves, ran down the stairs, and strode off down Curzon Street towards Golden Square.

Neville was right about another thing: Cecilia was at home, but she was not in her studio. Instead, she was in the front parlor doing absolutely nothing but gazing out over the square in front of her. The events of the last few days had left her thoughts and feelings in such a turmoil that she could not put her mind to anything except the confusing mass of emotions that continued to assail her.

She had gone from anger at what she considered to be Sebastian's betrayal of her trust, to her own shame over failing to act as promptly and rigorously as she should have where Neville and Barbara were concerned, to admiration for Sebastian's resourcefulness and determination at chasing after the runaway pair, to sorrow at the way he had said good-bye.

There had been something so final in his whispered *thank you* and the way he had kissed her hand, a finality that told her he would never again come to her studio just to talk to her or stop by his mansion in Grosvenor Square in the hope that she might be there in the ballroom working out measurements for her paintings. A finality that made her completely alive to the desperate passion of his kiss in the curricle as they chased after Neville and Barbara. It had been a kiss between two people who would never fulfill the promise of the special bond that had existed between them.

And it was that very finality—his clear acknowledgment of his commitment to Barbara, a commitment that could not allow Cecilia in his life—that made Cecilia admit to herself what her heart and her body had known for a long time now: that she was in love with Sebastian, and that there was simply nothing she could do about it except try to survive as best she could.

Undoubtedly, at some point, the insight she had gained from the experience, the joy and the suffering, would slowly come to affect her paintings, making her grow as an artist in ways she could never have imagined before. But for now, it quite simply hurt—slowly, exquisitely painfully, and excruciatingly hurt.

Then had come her brother's sudden announcement that Miss Wyatt was soon to become the Marchioness of Shelburne. Cecilia, whose emotions were already stretched to the breaking point, did not know what to do or think. Surprisingly enough, Neville seemed genuinely happy, and not just because he was marrying a fortune or because this proposal did not involve an uncomfortable journey in a badly sprung carriage, but because he truly enjoyed Barbara's company. And, struggle though she did against it, Cecilia could not help feeling just a little bit jealous of her brother's happiness.

So Neville had gone off to his club and Cecilia had continued to sit staring out the window, not knowing quite what else to do. In fact, she was so absorbed in her own confusing welter of thoughts that she did not hear the steps on the stairs or Tredlow's, "The Earl of Charrington to see you, my lady."

She did not hear anything at all until a deep voice spoke behind her. "Cecilia, are you quite well?"

"My lord!" She started and rose to her feet to find Sebastian smiling down at her in the way that had always made her heart feel as though it had taken over her entire body. "I am so . . . I mean, Neville has told me that . . . In short, I hope that you are not up—" She broke off suddenly, terribly afraid that she had been wrong all along and that he had actually cared for Barbara.

"You mean that Neville has told you he has saved me from a truly disastrous mistake I nearly made?"

"But I thought that marriage to Miss Wyatt was something you had considered quite carefully for some period of time. Surely—"

"I *did* consider it for a length of time, and when I made the decision to ask her to become my wife, I was completely convinced that it was something I truly wanted to do. But that was before I was in possession of all the facts."

"What facts?"

"Well, I don't suppose one would call love a fact, precisely, but it was before I knew that such a thing as love actually existed. But then, much to my joy and my sorrow, the unbelievable did happen: you came into my life and proved to me that love did exist after all. And all of a sudden I wanted nothing more than to spend the rest of my life with you. I, who had relished the idea of a coldly formal and comfortably distant marriage suddenly found myself wanting desperately to share my every waking hour with you. Feeling that way, I found the idea of being with her, or anyone else, worse than being alone. It was torture indeed.

"But now, thanks to your brother, it is a torture from which I am free at last, free to say I love you, Cecilia. I have always loved you, and I want you to become my wife. I want to be with you forever."

Cecilia's knees went weak and her hands began to shake, as the wave of happiness washed over her. It was true, then. He did love her. He had not loved Barbara. But as that first wave receded, the cold fear of doubt came swirling in its wake. What would it be like? What would being together forever be like, and what would it do to her, to the life she had tried so hard to build?

Other women had their husbands, their children, and their estates; she had her art. And she knew that much of her success in her field had come because she did not have those other distractions, because she had been able to devote herself to her career with a single-minded passion. What would happen to it if she developed another passion? Would it simply go away, wither up and die? And if it did, what would become of her?

No! She could not risk it. She could not throw it all away—all that was real and established—simply for the promise of love. She could not throw a lifetime away, no matter how much she wished at this particular moment to surrender herself completely to the wonder of newfound love.

"What is it? Why not?" Sebastian took her chin in a firm but gentle clasp, forcing her to look up at him. It was only then, when he held her head still, that she realized she had been shaking it *No, no, no.*

"I cannot," she whispered, her voice full of tears. "Please go and leave me. I cannot marry you or anyone."

"Cecilia," he pleaded, as tears filled her eyes and began to spill down onto her cheeks. "My love, just tell me why, and then I shall go. I will do anything that you want to make you happy, but please, let me know what it is."

"I . . . I must be alone. I cannot work if I am not alone. I cannot be like other people. My painting is all that I have," she wailed as the tears began to fall in earnest, and her body was wracked with sobs of despair. Why oh why did she have to discover love only to learn that it was impossible for her?

"My darling girl." Sebastian pulled her into his comforting arms and held her, gently stroking her hair until the sobs had subsided. "I would never, never do anything that would in any way take away from your painting or your career. How could I, when it was a picture of yours in the first place that taught me what love is?"

He smiled down at her bowed head. "Have you ever thought that perhaps being married might give you more rather than less time to devote to your art? You will have someone to share your responsibilities instead of having to shoulder them all by yourself. There will be someone else to take some of the burdens from you. I too share the same sort of worries. For years, it was my loneliness and isolation that were my strengths. They allowed me to focus all my energies on rebuilding my life and my fortunes. It was only after I had succeeded beyond even my expectations that I began to wonder what it was all for. Then I met you, and I knew the reason behind it. It was so I could truly live life. Just being able to share what little I was able to share with you inspired me. Knowing you made me want to be the very best that I could be—even better than I had been before."

Gently he released her, and taking her hand in his, he said, "Follow me."

"What?"

"I will show you what I mean." He led her down the stairs and into her studio, where he picked up her sketchbook. "May I?"

She nodded.

Slowly, carefully, he flipped through the pictures until he found the sketch of Cupid and Psyche. "There. See? That is not the way it looked when you first showed it to me. Then, it was still and lifeless. Now it is full of this." He cupped her face in his hands, bringing his lips down on hers, warm and demanding, sucking all the strength from her body until she was overcome with that desperate insatiable longing. He pulled her into his arms so that her body was molded against his, so that every beat of his heart throbbed in her veins, until there was nothing in the world but the two of them—no pots of pigment, no stacks of canvases or bottles full of brushes. Just the two of them consumed by the hunger and longing for one another.

And then, just as quickly as he had pulled her to him, Sebastian let her go. "You cannot say that you would have been able to fix this picture if you had not shared this with me," he whispered against her cheek.

He laid the sketchbook unsteadily back on the table where it had lain, but he was breathing so hard his hand shook, and it slipped and fell to the floor with a smack.

As he bent to retrieve it, his eye fell on another picture— the picture to which the sketchbook had opened when it fell—a picture of Samson, his sinewy chest bare, his chained arms straining at the pillars, his jaw squared, and his face set with determination. It was his own face. Sebastian's face lit with a fire and a pride that only love and complete understanding could inspire.

"Oh." Cecilia gasped, reaching vainly for the sketchbook, her face suffused with a self-conscious blush. "No." He held it up beyond her grasp. "It is good, my love, so very, very good. You are truly a lady of talent. But you cannot deny that love gives the inspiration that makes one truly great."

He looked deep into her eyes. "You once asked me if I thought it was honest to marry someone without loving them. I now ask you if you think it is honest to love someone without marrying them. And I promise you, I will only take no for an answer."

Then, not giving her any time to respond, he pulled her back into his arms and pressed his lips hungrily to hers until she could not think of anything at all.

Signet Regency Romance
by
Evelyn Richardson

The
Scandalous
Widow

0-451-21008-5

Available wherever books are sold or at
www.penguin.com

Now available from SIGNET REGENCY

Elizabeth's Rake by Emily Hendrickson and
Cupid's Mistake by Karen Harbaugh
Two stories of romance, seduction, and adventure
from two classic Regency authors—together in one
volume for the first time.
0-451-21431-5

The Lady and the Cit
by Blair Bancroft
In order to properly own her beloved lands, Miss
Aurelia Trevor needs a husband. Offering her hand to
the infamous businessman Thomas Lanning promises
him a seat in Parliament. But soon this marriage of
convenience turns to one of love.
0-451-21432-3

Available wherever books are sold or at
www.penguin.com

Allison Lane

"A FORMIDABLE TALENT...
MS. LANE NEVER FAILS TO
DELIVER THE GOODS."
—*ROMANTIC TIMES*

The
Madcap
Marriage

0-451-21095-6

Available wherever books are sold or at
www.penguin.com